DEATH SHIP

The ship was a floating holocaust. Sails were fireclouds spiked on flaming masts. Looming above was a mountain of orange-red smoke.

The *Bay* was a bomb with the fuse lit. Any second now, her secret cache of explosives might blow . . .

A mast toppled. The ship wallowed, rolling from side to side. Slocum was thrown across the deck toward the starboard. An explosion sounded, a dull concussion amidships, which was as much felt as heard . . .

He was booted off the ship into space. It was like being shot from a cannon. Hitting the water was worse. At the speed he was moving, it was like hitting solid ground. He skimmed across the waves, then sank.

JAKE LOGAN

SLOCUM AND THE PIRATES

J

JOVE BOOKS, NEW YORK

SLOCUM AND THE PIRATES

A Jove Book/published by arrangement with
the author

PRINTING HISTORY
Jove edition/June 1995

ISBN: 0-515-11633-5

A JOVE BOOK®
Jove Books are published by The Berkley Publishing Group,
200 Madison Avenue, New York, New York 10016.
JOVE and the "J" design
are trademarks belonging to Jove Publications, Inc.

PRINTED IN THE UNITED STATES OF AMERICA

10 9 8 7 6 5 4 3 2 1

SLOCUM AND THE PIRATES

1

On a night in late March 1882, the ship *Matagorda Bay*, a freighter that also carried a few passengers, was sailing off the east coast of Yucatán, a peninsula in South Mexico that sticks out like a thumb into the Gulf. The ship was out of Galveston, now on the last leg of her trip to the Yucatán port of Ciudad Aurora, the Dawn City.

At a little before midnight, Slocum left his cabin on the forward deck, starboard side. He stepped outside, locking the door behind him. He was a big man: broad-shouldered, long-limbed, and rawboned. He wore a wide-brimmed, low-crowned, straw planter's hat; a lightweight white suit; and boots. Although he wore no gun-belt, a six-gun was tucked into the top of his waistband at the hip. The front sight post had been filed off to prevent snagging. A jacket flap covered the gun, but not the bulge it made. A knife was hidden in his boot.

Slocum stood to one side of the door, his back to the wall, letting his eyes adjust to the night. Warm, moist, foggy darkness was everywhere. The deck pitched and swayed. Canvas flapped, lines creaked, boards groaned. Water splashed and hissed along the sides.

He was alone. He took a few deep breaths, filling his lungs with sea air. It tasted good, after the close confines of his cabin.

He went to the rail, looked out. Fog; fog and black water.

He started toward the bow. Lights burned in the cabin forward of his, shining through curtained portholes and slatted door panels. It was occupied by Don Pedro Mendoza and his beautiful young wife, Isobel; Mexican gentry en route to their ancestral estate near Aurora.

A murmur of conversation drifted out of the porthole, too low for Slocum to make out. He moved on, leaving no footfalls to mark his passing, a big man walking softly.

The next and last cabin in line was taken by the two Mendoza children and their duenna.

Slocum reached the bow and stayed there for a few minutes, watching the cutwater part the sea.

Turning, he went aft along the port side. Clouds of sail billowed overhead. Lanterns dotted the ship, caged globes of amber light.

At the waist of the ship, Slocum stepped into an alcove, out of the breeze.

The main cargo hold was amidships. Grilled covers were battened down over the hatches. Crates were piled high on deck, in rows. They were covered with tarps and secured by lines.

Slocum removed a cigar from an inside breast pocket. He rolled it in his fingers, holding it under his nose. It smelled good. He bit off the tip, spat it out. Some stick matches lay at the bottom of his jacket's right side pocket. He fished one out, pressing the tip of his thumbnail to the head to light it.

A figure came out from between the crates. Nichols, the second mate, a grizzled old salt. He wore a flat white cap with a stiff black visor. He crouched, holding a shotgun.

He looked like he was looking for someone. He didn't see Slocum.

Slocum cleared his throat. "Good evening, Mr. Nichols."

Nichols turned toward the sound, swinging the gun with him. "Eh? Who's there? Speak up!"

The twin bores of a double-barreled shotgun were leveled in Slocum's direction.

"Easy with that scattergun, Mr. Nichols. It's me, Slocum."

"Slocum, eh? Come out where I can see you."

Slocum stepped out of the shadows into a patch of lamplight.

Nichols was narrow-eyed, suspicious. "What're you sneaking around for?"

"Just lighting a cigar," Slocum said.

He thumbnailed the match head, flicking it to life. It flared with a hiss, underlighting his face. He set fire to the end of the cigar, puffing. It glowed orange. Smoke wreathed his head. Shadows reclaimed his face as the match played out.

He said, "Would you mind pointing that gun somewhere else?"

"I might," Nichols said. "What's your game, mister?"

"A turn on deck and a smoke, that's what I'm after. Is that a crime?"

"Maybe. It's ungodly late to be up and about—for honest folk."

"I haven't been sleeping too well on this trip."

"You ain't been well on this trip, period! Haw!"

Nichols's laugh was harsh, barking. He said, "Mostly, you've been one of the sickest lubbers I ever did see! First three days out, you were hung over the rail, heaving!"

Slocum said, "Yeah."

"Talk about seasick! Mister, you were pea-green!"

"I don't feel so good now, either. Not with that shotgun on me."

"Don't worry, I never shot nobody yet that I didn't mean to," Nichols said.

Still, he swung the muzzles down, pointing them at the deck.

"Guess it's okay. You seem harmless enough," he said.

"Thanks."

"But you shouldn't go poking around the cargo, mister, not in the dark. I might have taken you for a thief."

"I didn't. Go poking around the cargo, that is."

Nichols squinted. "No?"

"No," Slocum said.

"Well, I saw somebody sneaking around the cargo, that's for sure."

"Not me. I was up at the front of the boat."

"Bow. And the *Bay*'s a ship, not a boat."

"Anyhow, I ducked in here for a smoke and saw you. You were toting that shotgun like you meant business, so I sang out. That's all there is to it," Slocum said.

Nichols was puzzled. "If it wasn't you I saw, who was it?"

Slocum shrugged. "Damned if I know."

Nichols looked over his shoulder, uneasy. Behind him was a wall of stacked crates, about eight feet high. An aisle opened in the middle of them, running fore and aft. Light reached only a few feet into it, leaving the rest of the passage black.

Nichols turned, sticking his head into the opening. His shotgun, too. He stood crouched, alert, listening.

Slocum puffed his cigar. Nichols stepped back, away from the aisle mouth.

"Gone," he said. "Must have gotten away while I was jawing with you."

"He can't have gone far," Slocum said.

"Far enough. To the forecastle. He's safe there, among the crew. None of them will say who it was, damn their eyes! They're afraid!"

Slocum said, "Afraid of what?"

Ignoring him, Nichols grew thoughtful, worried. He fretted, grinding his jaws. Abruptly, a thought struck him, making him look up.

"What if it wasn't a crewman?" he said.

Slocum said, "It wasn't me, and it wasn't the Mendozas, I'll tell you that."

Not really listening, Nichols said, "Maybe it was one of ship's officers . . . I don't know. There's been some damned funny business on this cruise!"

That last remark seemed to snap him out of his gloom. His eyes were sharp, questing.

He said, "I'd advise you to get back to your cabin, mister. It's not healthy to go about on deck at night!"

"Or day."

"What's that supposed to mean?" Nichols's tone said he knew exactly what it meant.

Slocum said, "Three men dead since we left port. This ship sure is a wonder for accidents."

"Accidents? Ha ha!"

"If not accidents, what?"

Nichols opened his mouth to speak, thought better of it, and was silent. He looked over both shoulders before continuing.

He said, "I'll do my talking before a naval Court of Inquiry, and when I do, I'll tell plenty!"

"Such as?"

Nichols shook his head. "Oh, no. If you don't know—

and I'm inclined to think you don't, not with your lubberly ways—then I'm not going to tell you. You're better off not knowing."

"Fine with me. I'm not one to stick my nose in where I'm not wanted," Slocum said.

"Good. Go to your cabin, lock the door, and don't come out till we reach port. That's what I'd do if I were you, mister."

"Reckon I might, at that. Good night, Mr. Nichols."

Nichols moved off with no reply.

Slocum crossed to the starboard rail to finish his cigar. The last he saw of Nichols, the second mate was still prowling around the cargo area.

Slocum smoked the cigar down to a stub and flicked it into the water. A glimmer of light caught his eye, shining somewhere out to sea.

He leaned forward, peering through the mist. The light was gone.

The fog thinned, and the light reappeared, a pale yellow dot floating between sea and sky. It clung to the side of a tall dark shape emerging from the mist.

A ship.

The intruder had black sails. She was sleek, trim, low-slung. She kept pace with the *Bay,* sailing parallel to her.

Black sails: a sinister touch, suggestive of a funeral ship.

Somewhere on the *Bay,* eight bells tolled.

Midnight.

Slocum eyed the ill-omened ship. She changed course, arching inward on a path that must inevitably intercept the *Bay.*

No crewman sang out, "Sail ho!" That bothered Slocum. Where was the night watch?

From behind came a groan and a thud. Slocum turned, facing the cargo area. No one was in sight.

Slocum went looking for Nichols. Soft-footed, silent, he approached the mass of cargo crates. They bulked up big on the main deck, forming a squat, square-topped pyramid. A central aisle divided it in two. It ran fore and aft and was wider than the widest crate. Other aisles crossed it at right angles.

Slocum entered the aisle in the middle of the cargo area's starboard side. A few steps took him into darkness. Boxes rose above him, hemming him in.

He reached under his jacket, drew his gun. He advanced sideways, crablike, presenting a smaller target. His back brushed against crates. His white suit showed in the dark, but that couldn't be helped.

The path took a sudden sharp turn to the left. Slocum rounded the blind corner, holding his breath. He let it out upon finding himself alone on the other side.

The cargo area was a maze. The passage ran aft for a few paces, then jogged to the right. Another blind corner.

The turning opened on a short passage to the center aisle, which it met at right angles. The space was dark; light fell on the aisle beyond. A cap lay on the deck. Nichols's cap.

Slocum moved forward for a better look. He stepped on something soft, yielding. A body.

He crouched down beside it. The blood smell was heavy. The corpse lay on the deck its head turned to the side. There was enough light for Slocum to see the face: Nichols. The back of his skull was crushed. His shotgun was gone.

Slocum rose, keeping his head down, his gun ready. He had to watch his footing. The boards were slippery, wet with blood.

Something moved nearby, on top of the crates. It fell on Slocum, smashing him down.

• • •

Burke Noon, the *Bay*'s first mate, knocked on the captain's door. He was huge, with a frog's head and a bull's body. A navy cap with a narrow black bill covered his balding crown. A six-gun was stuffed in a hip pocket. A knife hung at his side.

The captain's quarters were below, at the stern. The door was closed. Light shone from the crack beneath the door. Outside, the passage was dim. Companionway stairs slanted topside.

Noon knuckled the door softly. It opened a crack. A gun stuck out of it at eye level, pointed at Noon. Noon blinked.

Behind the gun were the eyes of Captain Hoyt. They were bloodshot, watery, suspicious.

He said, "Noon! What do you want?"

"There's trouble, skipper."

"This trip's been nothing but trouble," Hoyt said.

If Noon was bothered by staring down the bore of a gun held inches from his face, he didn't show it. He looked sleepy, maybe a tad sulky.

Hoyt said, "Are you alone?"

"Yes."

"You'd better be," Hoyt said. "Step back."

Noon took a step backward.

"Farther," Hoyt said, "a good six feet away, at least. Hands where I can see them. No sudden moves, please."

Noon shrugged, stepped back. Hoyt opened the door, swinging it inward. He stood to one side of the doorway, peeking out from behind the wall. His face was flushed, his eyes glittered. He stepped into the doorway, clutching the frame for support. His gun hand shook; his knees trembled: not from fear, from drunkenness.

The captain leaned into the passage, looking around. He craned to see past Noon, who took up a lot of space. What he saw, or didn't see, must have satisfied him, for he stepped back into his cabin, motioning Noon to enter.

Still covering Noon, Hoyt backed up until he bumped into a desk. He sat on the edge of it, holding the gun in his lap.

Noon had to turn sideways to squeeze his broad hulk through the door. The stateroom was close, oppressive. A lamp hung from the ceiling over the desk, shedding a cone of oily yellow light. Beyond the light, the shadows were thick. Dim shapes outlined a bunk, a sea chest, and a tall glass-fronted cabinet. The air reeked of sweat, tobacco smoke, and alcohol fumes.

Hoyt said, "I had to make sure you were really alone, that no one was holding a gun to your back."

"Now you know," Noon said.

Hoyt nodded. "Which doesn't mean that I trust you."

"Hard words, from a skipper to his first mate."

"It's a hard world. Now, close the door and lock it."

While Noon obeyed, Hoyt went behind his desk and sat down. He held the gun resting on the desktop. Nearby stood an open bottle of rum and a glass tumbler. The tumbler lay on its side, rolling back and forth on its rim in response to the rise and fall of the ship. Rolled nautical charts massed at the sides of the desk, where they had been pushed out of the way.

Hoyt reached for the bottle, thought better of it, and stopped his hand a few inches short of its goal. He withdrew it slowly, reluctantly. He reached inside his shirt and scratched his chest.

Noon started forward. When he was midway between the door and the desk, Hoyt's gun rose to cover him.

Noon halted. His eyes were less sleepy, sulkier.

Hoyt said, "I've seen enough of what those big hands of yours can do. I have more sense than to let myself get within reach of them, Mr. Noon."

Noon allowed himself a show of resentment. "If I didn't knock hell out of troublemakers in the crew night and day, they'd have cut our throats a long time ago!"

"No doubt."

"Then why the gun? We're on the same side—"

"I hope so. But until I know for sure, I'm not taking any chances," Hoyt said.

Hoyt eyed the bottle, smacking his lips. His hand drifted toward it, as if of its own accord. At the last minute, it swerved, righting the overturned tumbler. It set the glass squarely in place, unhanded it, and withdrew. Fingertips drummed the desktop, then inexorably began creeping toward the bottle again.

Burke Noon laughed. Hoyt colored. He put his hand in his lap. His other hand motioned with the gun, a warning gesture.

Hoyt said, "Show some respect. Even a drunk can't miss at this distance . . . and you're a big target, Noon."

"Save your fight. You're gonna need it."

Hoyt frowned. "What's that supposed to mean?"

Burke Noon indicated the bottle. "Why pussyfoot around, skipper? If you want a drink so bad, take it."

"Never mind about that. You were saying . . . ?"

The mate was smug, silent. He stroked his fuzzy brown beard.

Click, went the hammer of Hoyt's gun as he thumbed it into place. "Mis-ter Noon," he said.

Noon stopped stroking his beard. He still looked smug.

"A ship," he said.

"What! A ship, you say?"

"Aye, skipper, and she's on our tail."

Hoyt's eyes narrowed. "Interesting . . . if true. I heard no alarm being raised."

"That's my doing. I don't want to warn any of their men

on board that the ship is near," Burke Noon said.

"You think there's spies among the crew?"

"What else? That explains everything that's happened this trip, all the fatal accidents and near misses. Funny how all the men who were lost were honest ones!"

"I can guess who the ringleaders are," Hoyt said. "Chino, Jim Gimp, and that fat monster they call Grouper."

Noon nodded. "The worst troublemakers on the *Bay*. Too bad you wouldn't let me handle 'em the way they should have been handled."

"How's that? By beating them to a pulp?"

Noon's lip curled. "Hell, yes! And turning them into fish bait the instant they got out of line."

"That's gotten you into trouble before, Noon."

"I know, or I wouldn't be on this tub." Noon sneered openly now.

"I'll see that you never have the displeasure of sailing on the *Bay* again," Hoyt said.

"Let's finish this voyage alive first, skipper. Or have you forgotten the stranger?"

"The other ship, yes. What can you tell me about her?"

"She's got black sails," Noon said.

"Black sails!"

Noon studied him with interest. "That mean anything to you?"

"No," Hoyt said, looking up at Noon. "You?"

"Black sails? No. Unless it's something like a black flag."

"Pirates fly under the black flag," Hoyt said.

"So I've heard."

Hoyt chewed his lips. "It means no quarter."

"Who expects mercy from a band of cutthroat pirates?"

"There's been piracy in these waters," Hoyt said. "Not often, but enough."

"It'll happen again, if we don't do something," Burke Noon said.

Hoyt, thoughtful, reached a decision. "All right. I'll have to trust you. After all, you're the most hated man on ship. Hardly a man aboard but wouldn't knife you with a smile."

"Yourself included?"

Hoyt grew stern. "The likes and dislikes of forecastle scum influence me not in the least, Noon. What I care about is how a man does his job, be he officer or ordinary seaman. When you give a man a beating, I can't get a full day's work out of him. That makes problems."

"It solves problems, too." Noon said.

Hoyt lay his empty hand palm down on the desk. "I won't argue. The point is, your overall loathsomeness makes you useful to me."

"Thanks . . . I think."

"If there's mutiny, those hellions in the crew will be after having your head, Noon. Mine, too. Which gives us a basis of mutual trust."

"That's too deep for me, skipper."

"Never mind. I'll take care of the thinking," Hoyt said. He was confident now, almost cocky.

Noon said, "By the way, captain, what do the ship's articles say about drinking on duty?"

It was a taunt, and Hoyt reacted instantly, stung. He slammed his open hand down on the desk. "Damn your impertinence, Noon!"

Noon said, "While you were drinking, I was acting. The crew's locked in the forecastle."

Hoyt's face was red, with hot, shining eyes. "By God, Noon, I've broken better than you—" He broke off, interrupting himself. "Eh? What's that you say?"

"The crew's bottled up."

Hoyt leaned back, owlish. "How'd you manage that?"

"Nichols spotted someone sneaking around on deck. A couple of us officers went looking for him. I spotted him going below."

"Did you see who it was?"

"No."

"Too bad!"

"Whoever it was, he ran into the forecastle," Noon said. "That lets him out. None of the crew'd inform on him. They're all too scared. Doesn't matter. I've got him, him and all the others like him hidden in the crew. As soon as I saw him take cover in the forecastle, I battened down the hatch. They're all trapped down there, spies and loyal seamen alike."

Burke Noon was smug. "How's that for thinking?"

Hoyt was enthused. It seemed sincere. "Good work, man! That gives us a fighting chance! At least we won't be fighting two battles, one on board and another against the intruder!"

Hoyt was full of plans now. He sat up straight, spine stiffened. He said, "We've two deck guns, one fore, one aft. A salute from them will show we mean business! Let's see . . . there's five ship's officers, the cook, Señor Mendoza—"

"That dandified Mex?" Noon interrupted.

"He can shoot," Hoyt said. "He's a sportsman and a hunter. With that family of his on board, he'll have plenty of reason to fight, poor devil!"

"That wife of his is worth fighting for. She's a beauty—"

"That's enough!" Hoyt spoke sharply, so sharply that he surprised himself.

At a lower, almost normal volume, he said, "Señora

Mendoza is a lady, Noon, and that's all that needs to be said about her.''

''She's got manners, which is more than I can say for some folks.''

''Mind your manners when you speak of your betters,'' Hoyt said. ''Anyway, Mendoza can be counted on in a fight. I'm not so sure of the other passenger, Slocum.''

Burke Noon stroked his chin. ''Slocum? I ain't sure what to make of him, myself.''

''He's no seafaring man. That seasickness of his wasn't faked.''

''He's Texas trash,'' Noon said. ''The cow towns are full of his kind. You can practically smell the manure on his boots.''

''I can't see him as a pirate.''

''Me, neither.''

''On the other hand, they do have cattle ranches in the Yucatán. So he could be what he claims to be, a speculator going to look into ranching opportunities there.''

''I never met a Texan who didn't know how to use a gun, so he might not be entirely useless in a fight,'' Noon said.

Hoyt said, ''Eight men, armed with Winchesters and Colts! The two women, the señora and her maid, can reload. We might even be able to let a few of the crew, the most trustworthy ones, out of the forecastle to handle ship's duties during the fighting!''

His hand plunged inside the open collar of his shirt, fishing out a flat brass key hanging on a chain around his neck. He pulled it off his head and held it with his fist closed around the top of the chain. The dangling key spun, glinting reflected light.

The gun remained in his other hand, as it had throughout the encounter.

He said, "Here's the key to the arms locker, Noon. Open it up and break out the weapons."

Burke Noon folded his arms across his chest. He said, "No."

"What?" Hoyt nearly shrieked.

"No, sir."

Hoyt was enraged. "Damn you, Noon, what are you trying to pull?"

"No more games, skipper. I know what's in the hold."

Hoyt pushed back his chair so violently that he narrowly missed upsetting it. He stood up, and this time the chair did go over, falling to the floor. Hoyt paid it no mind, his attention focused on Noon.

Noon didn't look worried. "Gunrunning's against the law. The *Bay*'s hauling enough firepower for a revolution. That could get you put up before a firing squad in Mexico, if you're lucky enough to ever reach port."

"Had to go poking around those crates, didn't you? Couldn't leave well enough alone, could you? Too bad, Noon."

Hoyt was working himself up. "The mutiny begins now, Noon, and you're the first casualty. 'Shot dead while attacking his captain.' That's how the report will read."

"Don't be stupid," Noon said. "You must know I've got a safety line."

Hoyt thought it over. "You're still alive. Convince me."

"The only time a skipper's as concerned with his cargo as you were is when he's smuggling something," Burke Noon said. "I followed you on one of your trips to the hold."

Hoyt gestured impatiently with the gun. Noon said, "I switched some of the boxes around. Hid a couple in a place only I know about. Not many, but enough for your buyer to come up with a short count. How're you going to explain it? Whatever you say, he'll think you stole the missing guns.''

"I'll find them," Hoyt said, sounding unconvinced.

"Don't be too greedy to live."

"Hah! That's funny, coming from you!"

"The pirates must know about the guns. Their spies on board know. I know. It's gotten too big for you to handle yourself, captain. You need a partner."

Hoyt sneered. "You, I suppose?"

"Who better? When there's a fight, I'm the man for the job—and there's a hell of a brawl coming."

Hoyt was scornful. "Damn you for putting me over a barrel when we're about to be attacked by pirates!"

"Can you think of a better time?"

"If they take the ship, you'll be as dead as I am, Noon."

"Right. So let's come to terms. Then we'll go fight pirates."

Hoyt said, "How much do you want?"

"Half," Burke Noon said.

Hoyt arched an eyebrow. Only half?" he purred. "That's all?"

"If I said I wanted less than half, you'd think I planned to steal it all later. If I said more than half, you wouldn't go for it. We split fifty-fifty."

"You're very generous with my money."

"You'll go along," Noon said. "Better half shares with me than a full share in Davy Jones's locker!"

He picked up the bottle, raising it to his lips. Hoyt grabbed for it, too late, saying, "Hey!"

"To our partnership," Noon said, and drank.

He took a long pull, throat muscles flexing as he upended the bottle. Hoyt had a stricken look. The bottle was lowered. Hoyt still looked stricken.

Noon smacked moist lips. "Ah, that's good," he said.

He saw the look on Hoyt's face and laughed. "Don't worry, skipper, I saved you some. Have a drink, it'll buck up your nerve."

Noon set the bottle down smartly on the desk. Too smartly, perhaps, for when he pulled his hand away, he knocked the bottle off balance, setting it to teetering on its base.

"Oops!" he cried.

Hoyt lunged, reaching forward with both hands, one of which still held the gun. Noon sidestepped, out of the line of fire. Gunmetal clinked against glass as Hoyt made a two-handed save, catching the bottle before it overturned. A few drops spilled.

Hoyt leaned forward, across the desk. Noon's hand covered Hoyt's gun hand. It lay on top of the gun so the loose skin between Noon's thumb and index finger was jammed under the cocked hammer. The gun couldn't shoot.

Noon plucked the gun from Hoyt's grasp. He freed the hammer, easing it down, then set the gun aside, on a corner of the desk beyond Hoyt's reach.

Hoyt smashed the bottle against Noon's head. It burst, spraying glass and rum. Not much rum; Noon hadn't left much. Much of the blow was absorbed by the folds of Noon's cap. Blood streaked the side of his face.

"Grrr," he said.

He grabbed at Hoyt, missed. Hoyt eyed the gun. It was too far away. He backed away, keeping the desk between him and Noon, careful not to get tangled up in the fallen chair.

Burke Noon's head hung down between his shoulders. He was breathing hard. Blood and rum striped his face. He looked out of furious pop eyes.

He put a hand on the desktop and vaulted feet first over it. He landed on the chair, breaking it into kindling.

Kicking aside the pieces, he bore down on Hoyt. Hoyt yelped. Noon grabbed Hoyt with both hands, lifting him off the floor and slamming him into the bulkhead.

Bones broke—Hoyt's. His ribs cracked. He couldn't draw a breath to scream. Noon drew his knife and thrust it into Hoyt's chest. It made a thunking sound. Hoyt wriggled. Noon hammered the pommel with the heel of his palm, driving the blade deep. Hoyt rose on tiptoes. The tip of the blade went through him, pinning him to the wall. Hoyt stiffened, then slumped, dead. He would have fallen, but the knife was holding him up.

Burke Noon shivered—not with revulsion, but like a dog shaking off water. The kill lust passed. A final shudder, and Noon threw off the last effects of the fit. His breathing was normal, his hands rock-steady, without a tremor.

His smile was a trifle loose and uncertain.

He pulled out his knife. It came free with a sucking sound. Hoyt slid down the wall and sat down, leaving a bloody smear to mark his passage. He fell over on his side and lay there, curled on the floor.

2

The attacker pounced. Instinctively, Slocum threw his arms
up over his head to protect himself. The man was on top
of him. Something swished near his head. Slocum slipped
in blood, losing his footing. As a result, the blow that was
aimed at the top of his head glanced off the side. It still
stunned him. It felt like the night had reared up and pole-
axed him, bludgeoning him with darkness.

He fell on his back, on Nichols, the body absorbing much
of the fall. The gun flew from his hand, skittering away,
lost. He got his bent legs up between him and his assailant.
The other was heavy, with thrashing limbs. Slocum grabbed
for his arms, in vain. The other struck, hammering a fist
downward. The man held a club, a belaying pin. The club
hit the deck near Slocum's head, so close that his teeth
rattled.

Slocum rolled to the side, straightening his legs. He
pushed the attacker off with his knees, slamming him into
a crate. The other grunted. He closed with Slocum. Elbows
and knees working, the two men clashed.

The other got on top, struck, clubbing Slocum's shoulder. Slocum grabbed his wrist, forcing the club hand down.

He elbowed the point of the other's chin, hard. It seemed to work, so he did it again.

The attacker spasmed. Slocum wrestled him to the side and down, still holding the clubber's wrist. The other man's knee worked frantically, slamming Slocum's thigh where he had turned it to protect his groin. Slocum crawled up on him, pinning him with his upper body. Now he was on top.

Slocum got a forearm across the man's throat. He pressed down, putting his weight behind it. The other man tried to snub his chin beneath the forearm, to protect his throat. Slocum had gravity on his side. His opponent was failing. Slocum ground out his resistance, his life.

Too late, the doomed man tried to cry out. All that emerged from his mouth were strangled, choking sounds. Slocum kept up the pressure. The other gurgled, heels drumming the deck. His feet were bare; they didn't make much noise. Slocum was relentless. The drumming quickened, peaked, then subsided.

The man's pounding heartbeats echoed against Slocum's chest. Finally, that drumming stopped, too.

The man stopped twitching. Slocum eased up, rolling off him. He got up on his hands and knees. Colored lights swam before his eyes.

Something hit him. At first, he thought it was the clubber, and that he'd have to fight him all over again. Then he remembered that the clubber was dead. What had hit him was the deck. Or, rather, he'd hit it, after temporarily blacking out. The impact of the fall had jarred him back to consciousness.

Not good. The fight had taken a lot out of him. If the clubber had friends, and if the friends should come looking for him, well, now, that was the end of Slocum.

He had to get away, go to cover until the weakness passed. And the gun—he had to find it. Without it, his chances were next to none. Gun. Getaway.

First, though, he'd have to keep from blacking out again.

Burke Noon opened the door, admitting three men to the captain's quarters. Jim Gimp looked like a scarecrow made of driftwood. He had stringy shoulder-length hair and a club foot. He used a crutch. He was a sailmaker and carpenter, compensating for his diminished mobility. Chino, the Mexican, was young, smooth-faced, with long, slanted eyes. Grouper was pale, flabby. Childhood disease had left him utterly hairless, eyebrows included. It made his head look like that of a fetus, except for the tattoos.

Jim Gimp looked around, saw the captain's body. He saluted it with an obscene gesture. Grouper said, "You were with him for a long time, Noon." His voice was piping, high-pitched.

"Sure, I was cutting a private deal with him," Noon said.

Grouper held up his hands, a placating gesture. He had thick fingers and pink palms. "I didn't mean nothing like that. We was worried something had gone wrong, that's all."

"Hoyt was cagey," Noon said. "It wasn't easy catching him off guard."

"Still, there he lies," Jim Gimp said, indicating the corpse.

"Yeah," Noon said. "Get rid of him."

Jim Gimp stayed where he was. Grouper and Chino went to the corpse. They turned out Hoyt's pockets, finding a watch but little else. The watch was a good one. "Gimme that," Noon said.

"I found it!" Grouper said.

"I killed him. Come on, hand it over," Noon said.

Grouper dropped the watch in Noon's outstretched palm.

Seeing that it was neither gold nor silver, Noon lost interest. He said, "You take it, Gimp."

Grouper said, "If you're giving it away, I'll take it!"

Jim Gimp made the watch disappear. "It's plunder, that's what it is, part of the loot to be shared out later. I'll hold it for safekeeping until then."

Noon said, "Quit squabbling and get back to work. Hoyt's bleeding all over my floor."

Grouper rejoined Chino. Chino laughed and said, "A shipful of guns, and you worry about a watch!"

"Yeah, well . . ." Grouper said, his voice trailing off. He and Chino each seized one of Hoyt's arms and dragged him across the floor.

There were windows in the bulkhead behind the desk. When they were opened, a puff of sea air filled the room, tangy, refreshing. The sound of the sea was louder, water gurgling under the sternpost. The open window framed a square of moist blackness marbled with drifting veins of gray fog.

The window had a deep casement. Chino and Grouper sat Hoyt in the window, holding him in place. His front was bloody from chest to knees. The knife wound was raw, ugly.

Chino and Grouper looked at Noon. Noon nodded. They let go. Hoyt fell backward, out of the window, brushing aside cobwebby strands of fog. A splash sounded; the top of a waterspout spiked into view through the window, then dropped out of sight.

Jim Gimp said, "With Hoyt gone, that makes you skipper, Noon. Congratulations, *captain*."

"The ship's not ours yet," Noon said, trying not to look pleased.

"She will be," Jim Gimp said. "With Hoyt and Nichols dead, and most of the honest fools stowed in the forecastle, we can pick off the rest one by one.''

"We've got the guns to do it," Noon said. He went to
the arms locker. Hoyt's key unlocked it. Inside were Winchester rifles, Colt six-guns, ammunition. Noon started
passing them out.

Grouper said, "Funny, us using these when there's a
whole hold full of firepower. Seems like going the long
way round.''

"Smuggled guns are packed in shipping grease," Noon
said. "Feel like cleaning them off in the middle of a mutiny?''

Grouper thought about it. "Uh, no.''

"Then shut the hell up and pass the ammunition," Noon
said.

The men worked. Tendrils of fog came creeping through
the window.

Slocum came to. Where was he? There was darkness, confusion. He floated . . . Shapes began to take form. He was
in a tight spot. He lay sprawled on the deck, wedged into
a narrow passage. Wood grain was rough against the side
of his face where it pressed the planking. Sense returned,
and with it, memory. He lay where he had fallen after
blacking out.

He rose to his knees, leaning against a crate for support.
His head felt numb. He couldn't tell where the top of his
skull ended and the night began. The two seemed to melt
into one another. He guessed it was the effect of the blow.
It was too dark to tell if he was seeing double. Awareness
kept fading in and out. When it faded out, fog took its
place. That scared him. Fear gave him a focus and pushed
the fog back.

He was himself again; for now, anyhow. How long he'd
stay that way was a question. He could feel the fog massing

at the edges of his mind, readying for the next assault. But for now, he could think, plan—maybe even move.

He looked around. Above him was dimness, indirect pearl-gray light filtered through mist that smoked and steamed. Outlined against it were the tops of walled crates. Behind, the passage continued for about six feet, then turned. Ahead, the path stretched into blackness. He was still in the cargo area, but where? He'd lost his bearings. The scene of the fight, was it near or far? He didn't know.

Behind was dimness; ahead, darkness. He turned forward, away from the light, weak though it was. He tried to walk but couldn't. When he stood up, fog rolled in. Next he knew, he was on hands and knees, head hanging down. He shook his head, trying to clear it. He bit his lip. That worked better, cutting through the haze. He chewed the inside of his mouth until the brain-fog lifted.

Crawling on hands and knees seemed to work. He made slow but steady progress forward. Darkness engulfed him. He brushed a shoulder against the wall to orient himself. There was a turning, then the path straightened.

He remembered the gun. Did he have it? He didn't recall picking it up, but then, he was not thinking too clearly. Pausing, he patted himself down. No gun. His jacket was gone, too. He had used it to mop off the blood that had gotten on him during the fight, to avoid leaving a telltale trail for his pursuers. That, he remembered.

He kept moving, crawling. A breeze fanned his face. His head lifted. Through a gap in the boxes, he saw open space. Instinct had made him seek the dark, shun the light. Now, he had won through. The maze was at an end.

The passage opened in the port-side corner of the cargo deck, toward the bow. Opposite it was a stretch of open deck bounded by the rail. Slocum was where he wanted to be, to port. The ship with black sails was approaching from the starboard.

A voice said, *"Pssst!"*

Slocum froze. He'd thought he was alone, but the voice was close. Again, it spoke: "Psst! Rip! You there?"

Slocum crouched, just inside the passage mouth. A man padded past, going aft, walking on the balls of his bare feet. He toted a long gun; a rifle or, more likely, a shotgun. His face was in shadow. He passed within inches of Slocum. If he had glanced to the side, he would have seen him, but his attention was fixed dead ahead.

A hand was cupped around his mouth as he called in a stage whisper, "Rip! That you, lad?"

From aft came a faint reply, too faint to make out the words.

"Rip?" Hope lifted the speaker's voice. His footsteps quickened as he moved aft, away from Slocum.

When Slocum looked again, the way was deserted. There'd never be a better time to make his move. Still, he hesitated. It was a desperate move at best. One misstep and he'd wind up at the bottom of the sea.

That decided him. If he stalled any longer, he'd lose his nerve. He started across the deck, toward the rail. He went on hands and knees to save his strength, what was left of it, and that wasn't much. Besides, he who walks small is less likely to be seen. If he was seen, he was as good as dead.

It was a long crawl to the rail. He gripped two bars and held on until the dizziness passed. He pulled himself up to the rail. The effort took a lot out of him. He lay across the top of the rail, hugging it, feet on the deck.

Commotion stirred on ship, spurring him. He threw one leg over the rail, straddling it. The other leg swung up and over. He stood outside the rail, facing starboard. Feeling carefully for footholds, he lowered himself over the side, out of sight.

Burke Noon and his three henchmen came up on deck. All were heavily armed, so laden with hardware that they clanked when they walked. They clustered at the aft end of the cargo deck.

They were joined by Cam Slattery, a scrawny, barefoot sailor with a shotgun. A dark woolen watch cap covered the top of his head, above a hard-bitten face. The corners of his mouth turned down. He said, "Rip's not with you?"

Noon said, "I thought he was with you."

"He was," Slattery said. "I lured Nichols while Rip jumped him from behind."

"Any problems?"

"None. It went off like clockwork. Nichols is done for."

"Good."

"We were looking for you when Rip thought he saw someone poking around the foredeck," Slattery said.

"Who?" Noon demanded.

"I don't know, I didn't see him. Rip did. He went forward for a look-see. I haven't seen him since. That was about ten, fifteen minutes ago. I was looking for him when I spied you men. Thought he might be with you."

"Well, he's not."

Slattery made no attempt to hide his unhappiness. "Where is he?"

"Damned if I know," Noon growled. "I've been busy with the skipper."

Jim Gimp said, "Cap'n Hoyt's fish food now, heh, heh, heh."

Slattery turned to him. "Did you see Rip?"

"Not me. Me and Grouper was standing guard outside the door, making sure no one interrupted Number One's chat with the skipper. Chino kept watch on deck. Did you lay eyes on young Rip, Chino?''

Chino shook his head. "I didn't see nobody."

Slattery rubbed his gaunt, stubbled cheeks as if trying to massage some life into them. "I don't like it. Where can he be?''

Grouper said, "Probably staking out his share of the loot for later."

"No, no, not Rip," Slattery said.

·Noon said, "Belay the chatter, there's work to be done. Gimme the shotgun, Slattery."

Slattery gave him the weapon. Noon broke it, making sure it was loaded. It was, both barrels. Noon expected no less. Nichols had been the conscientious type. So was Noon, in his way. That was why he had double-checked the piece.

He closed it, holding it one-handed by the stock. It looked like a walking stick by comparison with the size of the man. He told the others, "You know what to do. Let's go."

He started forward, the others following. Slattery hesitated, unsure. Jim Gimp said, "Don't worry about Rip. That brother of yours can take care of himself."

"I don't like it," Slattery said. But Jim Gimp wasn't listening. He'd already set off after the others. Despite his crutch, he moved swiftly, with a minimum of noise. Slattery, now alone, stepped off after him.

With Noon leading, the group swept forward along the central aisle of the cargo deck. Slattery lagged behind, gloomy and apprehensive. Beyond the crates was an open space, leading to the raised foredeck. The mutineers went forward, along the starboard side. Through the fog, the ship with black sails could be seen cleaving toward them. They climbed a short flight of stairs and skulked in a single file along the way to the passengers' cabins.

They split into two groups. Noon and Jim Gimp took one door; Chino, Grouper, and Slattery took the other. Lights burned in both cabins.

Jim Gimp loosed his crutch out from under him and stood on two feet. A wide stance maintained his balance. The crutch's curved rest that went under his arm was weighted with lead beneath its padding. It formed a cudgel heavy enough to break bones. He held the crutch in both hands, like a spear, its knobbed top leveled at the door.

Noon held the shotgun. The others waited for his signal. Noon grunted. That was enough for Jim Gimp. He thrust forward with the crutch, a short, savage blow that struck the door above the handle. The lock broke; the door flew open.

Inside was Don Pedro Mendoza and his wife, Isobel. He had dark curly hair, gray at the temples, and a thin mustache. He wore a smoking jacket of some rich burgundy-colored fabric, belted at the waist. He sat in a chair by the bedside, between the bed and the door. An open book rested on his lap. One hand was curved around a brandy glass. A bottle of brandy stood within reach on a side table. So did a gun.

Doña Isobel sat in bed, swathed in the frilly layers of a nightdress.

Don Pedro dropped the glass and lunged for the gun. Noon cut loose with a shotgun blast, catching Don Pedro in the chest.

Noon entered the room. The woman was too scared to scream or even to breathe. He spoke to her in Spanish.

"It was a mercy," he said. "This, too."

He fired. The blast all but cut her in two. Her face was untouched. Blood-spattered, yes, but untouched.

Jim Gimp goggled. *"Judas fire!* What'd you kill her for?"

"No survivors," Noon said.

"She could have died later! What a waste of prime womanflesh!"

"Woman on a ship's bad luck."

"Not when there's no cabin boys handy," Jim Gimp said.

Grouper shot the lock off Slocum's door, kicked it open. He and Chino fired into the room, emptying their six-guns before realizing that Slocum was absent.

Jim Gimp and Noon went out on deck. Screams and sobs came from the next cabin forward, the one housing the duenna and the two youngsters. Noon made a sour face.

Up came Grouper and Chino, their gun barrels smoking. Grouper said, "Slocum's not there!"

"Find him," Noon said. "And where's Slattery?"

Grouper and Chino looked over their shoulders, finding Slattery gone. Grouper said, "He was here a second ago."

Jim Gimp said, "Gone to look for his baby brother, I'll wager."

"Damn him!" Noon said. "Going off on his own at a time like this—!"

"Rip's his brother," Jim Gimp said.

"Damn 'em both! And damn Slocum, too, for not having the decency to stay put and be slaughtered like he's supposed to!"

"You're not worried about that lubber, are you, Noon?"

"He's a question mark, and I don't like it! I'll look into this myself," Noon said. He started aft.

Jim Gimp jerked a thumb in the opposite direction. "What about the nursemaid and the kids?"

Noon was blank faced. "You know what to do."

He shouldered past Chino and Grouper, descending the stairs to the lower deck.

Grouper smacked his lips. "I know what to do . . ."

"Sure you do," Jim Gimp said.

Grouper waddled to the forward cabin, trying the door handle, rattling it. The door was locked. His effort set off fresh wails from inside. They were shrill, hysterical. Grouper pulled out a pistol and shot the lock. He leaned on the door. It opened inward about six inches before bumping up against an obstruction. A steamer truck barricaded the door. It stood upright.

Grouper laughed, as if all this was great sport. He nodded, winking at Chino and Jim Gimp. He leaned harder on the door, putting his shoulder to it, pushing the trunk behind it. The door opened wider, and now he could see inside the room.

The duenna was a dish-faced older woman in a severe black bonnet and long-sleeved black dress. She stood against the wall, opposite the open door. She had thick brows, black-button eyes, a pug nose, and a tight-lipped mouth. Frowning with concentration, she held a metal object in both hands, pointed at Grouper.

In a far corner crouched the Mendoza youngsters, a boy and a girl, holding each other and crying.

Grouper paused, indecisive. The duenna's gun was a threat, but he didn't want to kill the woman. She was no prize, but she was female and it had been a long trip. He decided to shoot her in the leg, but she shot first.

Flame ringed the derringer's muzzle. A sharp report sounded simultaneously with a chunk of the door atomizing near Grouper's head.

Grouper's eyes widened. It had been a near miss. *But a miss is as good as a mile,* he mused, forcing his flabby bulk through the partially blocked door.

The duenna fired again. The bullet hit Grouper square in the middle of the face, extinguishing the light in his astonished eyes. He was dead on his feet, but so tightly was he wedged between the door and the frame that he remained upright for long ticking seconds. Gravity triumphed, sucking him down to the deck.

Chino laughed, an eerie trilling like the cry of a tropical night bird.

The derringer held two rounds, and now it was empty. The duenna later had cause to bitterly regret their loss. Not for herself, but for the children.

3

Rip Slattery's eyes bulged, as if amazed at finding their owner dead. An unlovely death: his face was black, his tongue stuck out, almost touching his chin, his neck was a mass of purple-black bruises where he had been throttled, his limbs were stiff. There was blood on him, but most of it belonged to Nichols, who lay nearby on the floor of the passage.

A lamp rested on the corner of a crate, shining down into the space. Cam Slattery and Noon stood inside the light, looking down at the corpses.

"The one called Slocum," Slattery said. "He did this."

"Could be," said Noon.

"It wasn't Nichols."

From the top of his forehead to the nape of his neck, the back of Nichols's skull looked like a broken honeycomb swimming in strawberry jam.

"If you'd hit him any harder, you'd have drove his chin to his nave," Noon said.

"He had a shotgun," Slattery said.

"I ain't kicking. Too bad you didn't do the same to that Slocum."

"Rip saw him. After we took care of Nichols, we went looking for the rest of you. Rip said he saw somebody walking around on deck. I didn't see anyone, but Rip was sure he had. He went back to check," Slattery said. "I should have gone with him."

Noon squatted beside Rip. "Strangled—throat's crushed. And Rip was a strong man."

Something glinted deeper into the passage, at the edge of the circle of light. Noon picked it up.

"What's that?" Slattery said.

Noon showed it to him: a gun. Slattery said, "It ain't Rip's."

"It's Slocum's." Noon ran a finger across the top of the bore. "Front sight's been filed off. Pocket gun. He must have lost it in the fight."

Slattery held out his hand. "Give it to me."

Noon shrugged, gave him the gun. Slattery pocketed it. Noon said, "One thing's sure: Slocum can't have gone far."

"I'll find him," Slattery said.

"Take him alive, if you can," Noon said. I want some answers out of him."

"You'll get them. I'm the one who has to write to our old gray-haired mother and break the news about Rip. Killing's too good for his murderer." Slattery patted Slocum's gun in his pocket. "Before I'm done with him, he'll be begging for a bullet from this."

Slattery turned, exiting the passage into the central aisle. As he did so, he nearly collided with Mahlon, another mutineer. Slattery was stone-faced, rigid. Mahlon was forced to step lively to avoid him. Slattery stalked off, leaving Mahlon to stare at his retreating figure.

Mahlon said, "What's the matter with him?"

"Death in the family," Noon said.

"Huh? I don't get it—"

Noon jerked a thumb at the corpse, silencing Mahlon. Mahlon crowded into the passage for a closer look. His shadow blacked out a third of the circle of lamplight.

He said, "Why—why, it's young Rip!"

"He'll never get any older," Noon said.

"Tsk, tsk. Slattery sure set a lot of store on that boy."

"That he did."

"Never much liked him, myself."

"Don't let Slattery hear you say that."

"He won't. He's gone. I know—I checked," Mahlon said.

Mahlon had sailed long years in the South Seas. His skin was burned bronze. He had a spade-shaped face, green eyes, pointed ears. The points were small but unmistakable. He wore a flat cloth cap and was swaddled in the depths of a navy pea coat. After the inferno of the South Pacific sun, a foggy night off Yucatán in the Caribbean Sea was too chilly for him.

Noon said, "What do you want, Mahlon?"

"The prisoners are on deck."

"They are, huh? Let's have a look at 'em."

At the mutiny's start, most of the crew had been locked in the forecastle. Later, the active mutineers freed the captives at gunpoint, releasing them one by one. They freed their cohorts among the crew first, doubling their numbers. The latecomers were armed like their friends with rifles and six-guns. They threatened to fire into the forecastle, massacring the loyalists among the crew if they didn't surrender. The remaining seven men had no choice but to submit. There were eight, but one of them had charged the hatch and been shot down through the bars for his troubles.

Honest seamen all, the seven now huddled on deck, miserable and forlorn. They had been beaten, kicked, cursed, and spat on by their erstwhile shipmates. They were bound hand and foot, clustered together.

They were guarded by three men: Mack had baby-fine blond hair, mild blue eyes, a curly golden beard. Gorgonios was squat, hairy. Lurkee was long and gangly, wedge-faced.

Noon arrived, with Mahlon in tow. Mahlon said, "There they are," meaning the prisoners. Noon barely gave them a glance. He glanced to starboard, where the black ship drew near. He said, "She'll be coming alongside soon."

Mahlon said, "Well"—also meaning the prisoners.

"You know what to do," Noon said.

Mahlon smiled, showing pointed teeth. They'd been filed that way, souvenir of a sojourn among Polynesian canni-bals. He drew his gun and started firing into the mass of prisoners. They screamed and shouted. Mack and Gorgo-nios drew their guns and joined in.

Lurkee sidled toward Noon. Noon watched him, heavy-lidded. Lurkee was hot-eyed, his horsey face set in stubborn lines. There was a lull in the gunfire. Noon said, "You ain't shooting."

"You, neither," Lurkee said.

"I give the orders."

"Yeah, well, I got a bone to pick with you, Noon."

"Yeah?"

"Yeah. Remember when you slugged me?"

"For insubordination. Captain Hoyt was watching. I had to make it look good."

"You knocked my tooth out. My jaw still hurts."

"You're lucky I didn't break your head, you damned fool!"

Lurkee, belligerent, thrust his jaw forward. His hand rested on the gun butt sticking out of the top of his pants. He said, "Maybe you'd like to try laying hands on me now, you—"

Noon threw a right jab, short and sweet. It landed on the point of Lurkee's jaw, slamming his teeth shut with a click. His eyes rolled up in the top of his head, showing only the whites. His head snapped back from the point of impact, his body following. He fell backward, measuring his length on deck.

Mahlon, Gorgonios, and Mack stopped firing to watch. Lurkee sat up, dazed. His eyes swam out of focus. He shook his head to clear it. His hand plunged toward his gun. There was the sound of a gun being cocked. Lurkee froze. His eyes focused. He saw the gun in Noon's hand. The hammer was raised and the bore pointed at him.

Lurkee raised his hands, shaking his head. "Let it pass, Noon." He spoke clumsily, through smashed lips. "I don't want no trouble. I'm backing off."

"Crawling, you mean," Noon said.

"If you want to call it that."

"Let you live to sandbag me another day? Hell, no!"

Noon fired, shooting Lurkee through the heart. The other three stared at him, careful to point their pistols where he was not. Noon spoke loudly, to be heard over the moans of mortally wounded captives.

He said, "Anybody else that's got a beef knows where to find me."

Mahlon, Gorgonios, and Mack, silent, reloaded and finished off the captives.

Jim Gimp came scuttling across the deck, moving as nimbly as a man with two good legs. A bundle was tucked under one arm. Taking in the scene with a glance, he said, "What happened to Lurkee?"

"I shot him," Noon said.

"What for?"

"Mutiny. Against me."

"Oh. Well, that's understandable. Lurkee was mighty sore about that beating you gave him."

"His complaint was noted and acted upon," Noon said.

"I see."

"More shares for the rest of us."

"More than you know," Jim Gimp said. "Grouper's dead, too." He told how Grouper had met his end, shot dead by the duenna.

Noon said, "I warned him his cock would get him into trouble."

"If this keeps up, you won't have much of a crew."

"I won't have much of a crew, no matter what, but they're all the crew I've got." Noon indicated the bundle. "What's that?"

"Here." Gimp handed it to him. It was a gun belt—two-gun belt. Holstered Colt .45s. The leather was well worn with use. So were the gun butts. Noon slipped the thong and drew one of the Colts. It fit his palm like it had grown there. The piece was well tended. It was heavy, weighted with lethal power. It seemed to vibrate from some internal gyroscope. Noon, thoughtful, slipped it back in the holster. It fit like a key in a lock.

He said, "Where'd you get this?"

"From a box under Slocum's bunk," Gimp said. "There was plenty of ammo, too.

"A gunman's guns. A professional, a *pistolero.*"

"What's he doing on the *Bay?*"

"Find him and I'll ask him, if he ain't dead," Noon said. I don't know which is worse, him alive or dead. Alive, he's trouble; dead, he can't talk."

Jim Gimp scoffed "Trouble? From a gunman without guns?"

"That's probably what Rip thought."

A wall of darkness loomed, the black sails of the intruder. The strange ship was closing fast.

Noon said, "Get rid of the stiffs." Mahlon, Mack, and Gorgonios grumbled as they set to the task. Killing was one thing, but this was work. Noon collared three more men, adding them to the detail. Two-man teams grabbed bodies off the pile, carrying them by the arms and legs to the portside rail and heaving them over. Sand from barrels was spread on deck to soak up the blood.

The dead went over the side, Lurkee included. Jim Gimp said, "There's two more on the cargo deck." Gorgonios and Mack hauled Nichols; Pablo and Duff lugged Rip Slattery.

The water boiled with sharks. Tiger sharks, striped, sleek, savage. Jim Gimp said, "They can smell the blood a mile off."

The sharks swarmed, dorsal fins slashing the surface, long muscular forms writhing. They churned the water with a tooth-gnashing frenzy. They tore corpses into shreds, then turned on each other.

More were arrowing to the site with every passing minute.

Nichols went over the side, raising a waterspout. Sharks descended on him. In an eyeblink, he came apart at the seams.

Pablo and Duff stepped up to the rail, young Slattery slung between them. Up dashed Cam Slattery, shouting, "Stop!"

He was waving a pistol. Pablo and Duff froze, still holding the body. Cam said, "Put him down."

Pablo and Duff set the body down on deck. Gently. Straightening up, they started to step back, preparatory to fading out of the picture altogether. This was not to be. Cam swung the pistol to cover them. Pablo winced and Duff rose up on tiptoes.

Cam said, "Cold-hearted bastards, treating a shipmate that way!"

Jim Gimp said gently, "What would you have us do with him, Cam?"

"My brother's not going to his final rest in a shark's belly."

"There's no fitter resting place for a sailor than the sea. Rip would have wanted it that way."

"Bullshit."

Then what would you be having us do?"

"Keep him."

Jim Gimp shook his head. "It's a hot climate, man—"

"He'll keep until we've sailed away from here!"

"He won't escape the sharks. They're everywhere."

"Then I'll bury him on land. On an island somewhere," Cam Slattery said. He got madder. "Try to stop me, and I'll put a bullet in you!"

"It's not worth getting shot over. Do as you please," Gimp said. He motioned to Pablo and Duff, shooing them away. "Git!"

They started to move off, Slattery glaring at them. Jim Gimp shifted his weight to his good leg. Suddenly he raised the crutch, swinging it upward at a ninety-degree angle. The tip struck the wrist of Slattery's gun hand with a swift, vicious blow, making a sharp crack. The crutch continued its upward arc, following through. The gun was knocked from Slattery's hand, sailing overboard. A shark caught it in midair, gulping it down.

Slattery reached for his belt knife. The crutch lashed out, striking him in solar plexus. All the breath in him was expelled with an explosive "Whoof!"

Slattery's face whitened. A gaping mouth filled the lower half of his face. He jackknifed, hugging his middle, then fell to his knees and stayed there, rocking, sucking air.

Jim Gimp said, "Sorry, Cam, but you would be a damn fool!"

Duff went over to Slattery. He was gnarly, potato-faced, dull-eyed. He said, "Point a gun at me, will you?"

He kneed Slattery on the chin, knocking him out. Slattery spilled onto the deck. Duff said, "Ow! My knee!"

He drew back his foot to kick Slattery. Jim Gimp said, "That's enough. You don't want to ruin him."

"Oh, don't I?"

"I said no." Gimp swung the crutch so that the tip was level with Duff's middle, pointing like a gun. Duff recoiled, wanting no part of it.

He said, "What the hell!"

Gimp said, "He put you under the gun and you paid him back. That's fair." The bottom of the crutch remained undeviatingly target on Duff's midsection.

Duff said, "Okay—okay!" Gimp lowered the crutch. "But it ain't fair," Duff added.

Mack had watched the scene play out. He said, "Noon killed Lurkee for less."

Gimp said, "We've lost enough men. We're short-handed as it is. Drago's crew already outnumbers us."

That was the clincher. The others nodded. Mack muttered, "There's sense in what you say."

Duff was the last to be convinced. "When Slattery comes to, Gimp, he'll be after both our hides!"

"We'll keep him tied up till he comes to his senses."

"Suppose he don't? What then?"

"We'll deal with that when the time comes," Gimp said. You can't blame him for being a little out of his head. After all, Rip was his brother."

Rip was shitbird. He got what was coming to him. He'd have gotten it long ago, if not for big brother Cam," Duff said.

"Since you feel that way, you'll be glad to see the last of him," Gimp said. "So hop to it! You, too, Pablo."

Duff grabbed Rip's ankles, Pablo held his wrists. Pablo said, "I no like him, too."

"Shut up and lift," Duff said. They swung Rip, pendulumlike, and heaved him over the side.

The sharks liked him.

4

The black ship came alongside *Matagorda Bay*. The stranger's crew lined the rail; hard men, heavily armed. They stood silent, in contrast to the riotous sailors on the *Bay*.

Grappling lines were used to secure the ships together. A gangplank bridged them at the waist. Three men crossed over from the black ship to the *Bay*. Captain Drago, Rector, and Emiliano Monte. Drago was master of the black ship, Rector was his bodyguard, and Monte was the ship's gunner.

Noon and Jim Gimp parlayed with the newcomers on the foredeck. Drago was tall, handsome, robust. He wore a plumed hat, an unbuttoned navy blue tunic with gold epaulets, tight breeches, and thigh-high soft leather boots rolled above the knees. A scarlet cummerbund circled his middle. Two pistols were stuck in the top of it. Hanging in a scabbard at his side was a three-foot sword. Rector was thin, bony, a transplanted Northerner with raw red sunburned skin and pale watery eyes. He wore a round, flat-brimmed hat, a thin, high-collared long black coat, and a gun belt with two guns, low-slung, tied down gunfighterstyle. Monte, the gunner, had curly hair and a beard. Where his bare face showed, it was pitted from being struck by high-speed particles of exploded gunpowder vented during cannon fire.

Drago waxed the tips of his mustache to make them stand point upright. A waxy, perfumed scent wafted from him. Noon moved to windward of him to avoid it.

Drago said, "You have done well, Señor Noon."

"Captain Noon," the other said quickly. "She's my ship now."

Drago sucked his breath between his teeth, making a whistling sound. "Yess, that is true. Congratulations, *capitán*."

"Thanks." Noon's flat, even tone suggested that Drago's acceptance of his new found status was of little importance.

Emiliano Monte fidgeted, impatient. "When do we get to see the goods?"

Drago laughed. "Can't wait to get your hands on those new toys, eh?"

Rector, silent until now, sniffed the air. "I smell smoke," he said. "What's burning?"

Eel and Aarn prowled belowdecks, searching for survivors who might have escaped the slaughter. Eel was gangly, with a long thin face and wavy blue-black hair worn close to the scalp. Aarn was husky with a broad, open face.

"This manhunting is hungry work," said Aarn. Eel agreed. They went to the galley in search of a snack. First, they entered the mess. It was empty. Aarn said, "I wonder what happened to the cook?"

"I shot him," Eel said.

"What'd you do that for? He cooked some damned good chow!"

"I caught him trying to set fire to the ship."

"Oh," Aarn said. "Too bad. He sure could cook."

At the opposite end of the room, a swinging door connected to the galley proper. Eel palmed it open, smacking his lips. He said, "I can taste them eats now."

The galley was in disarray. Cabinet doors hung open. Pots and pans lay scattered about. Bloodstains marked the walls and floor, glistening wetly. Eel looked around, not finding what he sought. Face darkening, he said, "Gone!"

"Who's gone?" Aarn said.

"The cook! He wasn't killed dead after all," Eel said, drawing his gun and plunging forward. "I'll fix that!"

He followed the blood on the floor and Aarn followed him. The trail wound through the bowels of the ship, leading to a door to the center hold. It was ajar, a bloody handprint stamped beside it on the door frame. The doorway was outlined with red light. Streamers of smoke crept out of the top, snaking along the ceiling of the outer passageway.

Eel cursed. He opened the door and flung himself into the hold. Heat and smoke struck him. The cavernous space was thick with flames. Behind him, Aarn's heavy feet clattered down the short flight of stairs to the hold, only to falter after advancing a few paces into the inferno.

A charred husk lay curled at the heart of the blaze, the remains of the cook. Mortally wounded, he had dragged himself here to die. Beyond the flames, singed by the heat, lay a now empty cask of oil with which he had drenched himself and his surroundings before applying the torch. It rolled back and forth with the ship's movements.

Smoke pawed Eel, making his eyes water and his lungs itch. He held his breath. A tongue of flame lashed out at him, so quick and fierce that he had to duck to avoid it. It singed his hair and showered him with sparks. He batted away the embers, brushing them off his head and shoulders. He knelt on the floor, coughing.

A blast of hot air sucked the moisture from the surface of his skin. Burning timbers hissed, spat, and popped. Black smoke massed under the high ceiling, coiling, thickening, underlit by coppery firelight.

Eel glanced back over his shoulder at Aarn, who had retreated to the foot of the stairs. Their eyes met. They both had the same thought: only they two knew that Eel's failure to finish off the cook had doomed the ship.

Both had guns in their hands, which they fired. Aarn missed, bullets flying over Eel's head. Eel knelt with his back to Aarn. He reached around his front with his gun hand, raised his left arm, and fired under it. A slug knocked down Aarn. He sat down, hard. Eel emptied the gun into him.

Smoke wisps curled from the floorboards. They grew warped from the heat. Eel shrank from them; they were hot to the touch. He crawled toward the exit, fast.

The cargo deck was lined on both sides with access hatches connecting with the hold below. Their square-shaped housings protruded above the deck. Gorgonios knelt beside one, studying it. Nearby stood Chino and Mack.

"Smoke comes from here," Gorgonios said. The hatch cover was closed. He reached for the batten to open it, then snatched his hand back with a gasp.

Mack said, "What's wrong?"

"It's hot," Gorgonios said.

"Hot?"

Gorgonios wrapped a kerchief around his hand. He began undoing the hatch.

"Maybe you'd better not," Mack said.

Chino shrugged, bored. "Open it."

Gorgonios undid the fastenings, hooked a hand under the lip of the hatch cover, and lifted it. An air seal popped as he wrestled off the cover, freeing the shaft.

It was like lifting the lid off Hell. The fire in the hold had already consumed much oxygen, creating a partial vacuum. With the hatch raised, air rushed in to feed the blaze. Gorgonios had to hold onto the housing to keep from being sucked into the shaft.

Fresh air fueled the blaze, turning the hold into a kind of blast furnace. A loud *crump!* sounded as the flames grew tenfold.

Fire jetted from the open hatch, vomiting skyward. Gorgonios, caught in the blast, became a human torch. Screaming, he threw himself over the side into the sea.

Fire at sea is a sailor's great fear. The *Bay*'s mutinous crew cried out at sight of the blaze. Fire and smoke vented through the open hatch. Other housings smoked like chimneys, their lids swelling, cracking, and peeling. One, two, many lines of smoke rose from the main cargo hatch. Crewmen dashed about in mass confusion.

Drago said, "This is not well." His tone was bleak.

Rector sought, caught his captain's eye. Waited for his cue. Drago shook his head, signaling *No, not yet.* Rector nodded, the anticipatory gleam fading from his eyes. A subtle exchange, almost imperceptible, but Noon had caught it.

He didn't like it, but before he could do anything about it, Eel stumbled into view, soot-blackened and scorched at the edges. Escaping from the hold, he had emerged through a door to the foredeck. He staggered a few paces and collapsed. He lay on his side, coughing and wheezing.

Noon went to him, jerking him to his feet as if he were a rag doll. His face was a mask of wrath. Eel saw his death there. Noon shook him, rattling Eel's bones.

Noon said, "Who did this? *Was it Slocum?*"

"No, no!" Eel spoke in a rush, to avoid another shaking. "The cook set the fire!"

"The cook!"

Noon roared. He held Eel at arm's length, in mid air. He shook him. "The cook!"

The shaking stopped, leaving Eel's eyes out of focus. He saw triple. Three faces of Noon whirled across his field of vision. Eel squeezed his eyes shut. That helped, some.

He said, "The cook got away from Aarn killed him torched the ship—"

"The cook!" Noon, furious.

Eel opened his eyes. "Killed Aarn and almost got me but I got him first! You must have heard the shots!"

Noon held a fist under Eel's nose. "Wait," Jim Gimp said. "I did hear some shooting before the fire."

Eel said, "The fire was already going when I got there. I almost got burnt up myself!"

Gimp said, "But where would cook get a gun?"

"He knifed Aarn and stole his. Tried to kill me but I got him first. Left him burning, the bastard!"

Noon flung him away. Eel hit the deck, took a few bounces, and rolled to a halt. Noon said, "The cook!"

He made a gesture of washing his hands, turned to find himself being eyed by Drago and his two associates. Drago tsk-tsked with mock sympathy, saying, "A most unfortunate setback, *capitán.*"

"I ain't whupped yet," Noon said.

He went to the cargo deck and waded into the crew, kicking and cuffing them into some semblance of firefighting order. But the blaze was well advanced.

The main hatch cover collapsed into the hold, freeing a genie of fire, which climbed into the rigging. It fell back into the hold, but the damage had been done. Now the upper works were alight.

Drago and his men made ready to leave the ship. Noon found them at the gangplank bridge. Gunner Monte had already crossed over to the black ship. He moved among the crew, ordering them to prepare to cast off. They hopped to it, eager to be free of the burning *Bay*.

Noon said, "We can cut the masts, flood the hold—save cargo and ship!"

"Before the fire touches off the explosives hidden in the hold? I think not," Drago said.

"But the cargo, man! The guns, the bombs—"

"Lost, all lost," Drago said sadly. "The great work must go on without them. Ah, well, at least our enemies shall not have them . . ."

He stepped up on the gangplank. "You and your men are welcome on my ship, *Capitán* Noon."

Scraps of burning canvas, embers, and soot rained down. "Pray, do not tarry," Drago said. He crossed the bridge to the other ship.

Rector went last, walking the narrow plank with ramrod-straight back and hands hanging loosely at his sides, near his guns. Noon glared after him.

"Snotty bastard," he said. He made sure Rector couldn't hear it.

Jim Gimp tugged at his sleeve, saying, "It's damned hot!"

Noon, sour-faced, fired his gun in the air to attract the attention of his men. When he had it, he put his hand to the side of his mouth and bawled, "Abandon ship!"

The mutineers quit the *Bay* for the black ship. Some crossed by the boarding bridge, some swung across on lines. A few tried to jump the gap. One made it. The others fell between the ships and sank from sight.

Cam Slattery was bound hand and foot, with a few extra strands wrapped around his middle. Pablo slung him over a brawny shoulder and toted him across the bridge. Slattery hung head-down from the other's back, looking back at the

Bay. Suddenly, he began to shriek.

Pablo said, "Shut up or I drop you."

Slattery kept shrieking. Pablo kept on going, bowed under by the weight of his burden. His active burden. He reached the other end and dumped Slattery on the deck of the black ship. Slattery hit his head and was silent.

The *Bay*'s decks were empty of all save the dead. The last of the mutineers were safely aboard the black ship. The boarding bridge was raised and the lines holding the ships together was cut.

For a heart-stopping moment, the ships cleaved together, side by side. Slowly, the black ship began to pull away from its fiery companion. Wind filled black sails, widening the gap.

Noon and Jim Gimp stood at the rail, watching the *Bay.* She was a pyramid of fire, bobbing on the face of the deep. Armaments lodged in her innards exploded. She blew up.

Matagorda Bay tore herself apart in a series of fiery blasts, a spectacular fireworks display.

When it was done, Jim Gimp said, "Looks like you ain't captain no•more, Noon."

"Grrrr," Noon said.

The *Bay* had two figureheads. One was a wooden statue of a half-nude woman adorning the ship under the bowsprit. The other was Slocum.

He straddled her back. She was seven feet tall, a giantess. She leaned forward, arching her upper body above the waves. Arms reaching out, hands held palm upwards. Round, weathered limbs. Wavy hair and a broad, bare back. From the waist down, she was fastened to the bow. Securely, Slocum hoped. She'd been making ominous creakings from the moment he'd first mounted her. So far she'd held, but still . . .

Earlier, he'd lowered himself over the side to a ledge. It was about six feet below the deck and three feet wide. It ran along the hull. Rigging was secured to it in places. He'd seen it plenty of times before, while being sick over the rails. He followed it to the bow, crawling on hands and knees. He swung a leg over the figurehead's back and straddled her. It squirmed beneath him and the bottom of his stomach dropped out. He feared he'd ride her to the bottom of the sea. But she was only settling under his weight and the shifting stopped almost as soon as it started. He eased as far back as possible, hoping to take some of the strain off. Below, waves hissed and foamed as they tore themselves in two on the cutwater. Above, the overhanging bowsprit wrapped Slocum in blessed shadow, hiding him.

His thighs hugged the statue's hard wooden flanks. Once or twice he blacked out, coming to a split second later as he fell forward. He was wedged in too tightly to fall off. Topside, the slaughter raged on. Sailors flung corpses to the sharks but didn't see Slocum, screened by the swelling curve of the bow.

Then came the fire. Slocum saw the flames reflected in the water. The fire grew, seeming to set the deeps ablaze. They were already red with blood. The sharks added an appropriately hellish note. Shouts turned to screams as the fire spread. Slocum laughed. Wait till the heat detonated the smuggled explosives! Not that there was much in it for him . . .

The mutineers abandoned ship. Slattery, carried slung over Pablo's shoulder, saw Slocum. Hanging head-down, he glimpsed a flicker of movement at the bow, as a man-sized blur ducked back into the shadows. In a single blinding flash of intuition, he knew, *knew* that lurking under the bowsprit was the man who had killed his brother. He

shouted his discovery, shrieked it, but his ravings were unintelligible to Pablo.

The black ship began to move, gliding forward. Firelight
picked out her name, written in gilt letters on her bow:
Perla Negra. Black Pearl.

She veered to starboard, away from the *Bay*. Slocum dis-
mounted from the statue, clutching a length of chain for
support. Footing was dangerous. His boots were clumsy,
slippery. Should have gotten rid of them before he started
climbing. Too late now. Hugging the bow, he edged along
the ledge, keeping the ship's curve between him and the
Perla Negra. When the black ship was well away, he
climbed the chain to the deck.

He was glad for the boots now. The deck was hot underfoot. The ship was a floating holocaust. Sails were fireclouds spiked on flaming masts. Looming above was a
mountain of orange-red smoke.

The *Bay* was a bomb with the fuse lit. Any second now,
her secret cache of explosives might blow.

The lifeboats were smashed, their bottoms stove in. A
parting shot from the pirates.

A mast toppled. The ship wallowed, rolling from side to
side. Slocum was thrown across the deck toward the starboard. An explosion sounded, a dull concussion amidships,
which was as much felt as heard.

Slocum ran for the rail. Nearing it, he glimpsed a pathetic
sight: the violated bodies of the Mendoza youngsters and
their duenna. He jumped on the rail with both feet as the
next blast struck.

He was booted off the ship into space. It was like being
shot from a cannon. Hitting the water was worse. At the
speed he was moving, it was like hitting solid ground. He
skimmed across the waves, then sank.

He surfaced, coughing and choking, treading water. He

retched up a mass of seawater, his lungs and sinuses burning. A wave struck him in the face, pouring another quart or two into his open mouth.

Explosions popped like firecrackers as the *Bay*'s contraband cargo blew up. A giant, invisible fist grabbed Slocum and squeezed him in the middle, so that it seemed that his guts must burst and his lungs pop from the pressure. That was the effect of a blast shock wave being transmitted through the water. The fist squeezed again and again as more blasts came. Slocum's limbs thrashed.

Matagorda Bay disintegrated in a fan-shaped burst of yellow-white light. Debris rained down, railroad-car-sized chunks and spidery high-speed slivers and all sizes in between.

The blasts subsided. Slocum felt as if he'd been beaten over every square inch of his body, inside and out. He was very very weak. It was all he could do to keep afloat.

What remained of the *Bay* was snapped in two, broken at mid-keel. Both halves started to sink. Slocum swam away from the wreck. Splashing feebly, he made but little headway.

The wreck opened a hole in the sea, a whirlpool. Ripples spiraled out from it, extending ever-reaching arms. They snatched up flotsam, spinning it, sucking it to the center of the vortex.

The current tugged at Slocum, trying to draw him back. He swam harder, calling on what little he had left. For a while, it was touch and go. His last reserves of energy ebbed and faded, but so did the current. The whirlpool slowed, shrank, swallowed itself up. The hole in the sea dimpled, vanished.

Perla Negra was nowhere in sight. Slocum was alone, surrounded by darkness and the deep. Wreckage bobbed about on all sides. He picked the largest piece and paddled toward it. A square-topped hulk, it wallowed in the troughs of the waves. It was farther away than he'd thought. He swam and swam, but it seemed no nearer. His limbs were stiff and his sides ached. He floated as much as possible. At least there were no sharks about. The blasts must have scared them off. Remembering them, he found a few extra ounces of strength he hadn't known he had.

He reached the hulk and climbed on top of it, out of the water.

5

Slocum was adrift on a sky-blue sea. His life raft was a piece of the *Bay*'s deck, a corner section that had survived the blast more or less intact. Most of it was submerged. The part that rose above the surface was about the size and shape of a farmhouse roof. Its slanted sides were knobby with stepped ledges and jutting beam ends. They sloped gently down to the water. Sprawled across the top lay Slocum.

At dawn he awoke. By midmorning, he'd recovered enough strength to sit up and survey his kingdom. On all sides, open sea stretched out to the horizon, unbroken by ship or shore. Calm sea, small waves. Strewn all about was a broad band of wreckage from the *Bay*. Blue water. Not the rich royal blue of deep ocean, but the blue of a robin's egg. The sky was hazy, humid, pale in comparison to the sea. Steamy clouds veiled the sun. It was hot.

The raft was solid, stable, seaworthy. It seemed in no immediate danger of sinking or capsizing. Its studded sides offered plenty of handholds, footholds, places to roost. Near the top was a narrow ledge on which he could lie down and stretch out.

He wore shirt and pants, that was all. The rest of his clothes had been shucked off during his desperate swim for life. His knife was gone, lost when he'd kicked off his boots to keep them from dragging him underwater.

He was hurting. He ached from head to toe, but nothing seemed to be broken. He was weak. He wasn't hungry, not yet, but he was thirsty. His lips and the inside of his mouth were encrusted with dried sea salt. He wiped his lips with the back of his hand, but could do nothing about the bitter, brackish taste in his mouth. It hurt to swallow. He had no food and no fresh water.

He asked himself, *Now what the hell do I do?*

Nothing much, came the reply. *Stay alive and hope for the best.*

The sun climbed higher, burning off the haze. Its shattered reflection was mirrored by countless wavelets, turning the sea into a field sown with dazzling crystals, glinting diamond-bright. Not so much as a breath of a breeze stirred the still air.

Sunlight beat down on Slocum's head until it seemed that his brain was boiling in the cauldron of his skull. He tore a sleeve off his shirt at the shoulder and ripped it in half. He dunked it in the water and wrapped it around the top of his head. It gave him some small measure of relief. When the head covering dried, he undid it, dipped it in the water, and retied it. The trouble was, it dried too fast, necessitating frequent trips down the side of the raft to the place where water lapped it. A knoblike projection served as a perch a few feet above the sea. He stayed there, reaching down to rewet the head covering as needed. Sweat poured out of him, marking the slanted planks against which he leaned with a man-shaped imprint.

Now that the sun was overhead, he cast no shadow. Its rays clarified the water, allowing him to see downward for several fathoms. There was motion there, murky clouds that flitted up, down, and sideways, suddenly coming apart only to reform and begin the dance anew. Schools of small fish, Slocum realized.

That gave him an idea. He would act on it later, when the sun had declined from its noonday height. Now it was so hot that to draw a breath caused him to break into fresh sweat.

The sun passed its zenith. Shadows stirred, crept, and grew. Slocum forced himself to move. He missed his footing and fell into the water. The plunge revived him. That, and fear. He hauled himself back onto the raft and lay there, panting and dripping.

He cursed himself for his clumsiness. Now he had frightened away the fish! But the dunking had helped cool him off and clear his head, giving him the strength to put his plan into motion.

He took off his shirt and wrung it out. He draped it over the top of the raft, out of harm's way. The raft bristled with jagged edges where it had been blown off the ship. Slocum went to work on the splintered end of a plank, tearing off one- and two-foot-long shards, widening the gaps in the wood. Splinters pierced his palms, but he ignored them. Where the wood was too thick to pull apart, he pounded it with hands and feet, shivering new cracks along the grain. When the fissures were wide enough for him to reach inside and get a handhold, he grabbed it and leaned back, putting his weight into it. Muscles corded, standing out as he strained against the board where it was nailed to a beam. He sat straddling the top of the raft, hands hooked under a long, wide tongue of wood.

Ordinarily, he could have snapped the board with a shrug of his shoulders, but not now, in his weakened condition. He trembled with effort but the board was unmoving. *I'll break it or my back,* he thought.

With a squeal, the nails came loose. Now freed, the board arched upward and back, snapping off a few inches inward from the beam. The sudden release of tension unbalanced Slocum, almost causing him to topple backward. His thighs gripped the sides of the raft, hugging them. He'd ridden too many wild horses to be thrown that easily, but he nearly dropped the board in the upset.

His heart pounded. Spots danced before his eyes. Holding the board to his chest, he leaned forward, head down, until the dizzy spell passed.

His prize was a strip of wood, about four feet long, six inches wide, and two inches thick. It was jagged at both ends. Three long nails protruded near one end, where they had been torn loose from the beam. They were curved and rusty, like bloody claws.

The raft floated on, serene and undisturbed by Slocum's action, which had barely raised a ripple. It would take much more than that to destabilize its massive equilibrium.

Slocum turned his attention to the shirt. It still had one sleeve. Using the nails on the board as tools, he tore off the sleeve, then shredded it into a number of long, thin strips.

He had saved the smaller pieces of wood that he had broken off earlier. Now, he picked three that were best suited to his purposes. They were each about eighteen inches long, varying between one and two fingers thick. Using some of the cloth strips, he tied the ends of the sticks together, forming a triangle shape. He tied one apex of the triangle to the nail end of the long stick. A study in concentration, he sat hunched over his work, fat drops of sweat falling from his face. The apex of the triangle was wedged between the nails for extra stability. He'd considered hammering the nails into the wood itself, but rejected the thought for fear of splitting the thinner sticks. But the nails served as anchors with which to secure the bindings. He wet the strips and twirled them before tying them in place. He doubled them for added strength, and bit down on the ends to pull the knots extrà tight.

The triangle-and-stick combination was crudely spoon shaped. Slocum laid his shirt open flat on the triangle. He left a hand's breadth of material hanging outside the framework on all sides as a border; the rest was massed inside. He speared the inner edge of the border of the sharp ends of the triangle points. A six-inch sliver of wood served as a hole puncher, scoring a line of regularly spaced holes on the fabric inside the framework.

He took a cloth strip, knotted one end, and threaded it through one of the holes. He tied a loop around the framework, snugging the shirt border to the wood. He threaded the strip through the next hole in the shirt, passed it over the top of the wood, then repeated the process at the next hole. Through the hole, over the top, under the framework, through the next hole, and so on.

When the strip neared its end, he knotted it in place, picked up a new strip, and started all over again. Working his way around the framework, he strung the border of the shirt to the triangle. The fabric hung down through the hole, forming a sack. A long-handled cloth sack.

A net.

Fish swarmed around the underside of the raft. Slocum crouched near the water's edge. He'd torn off his pants' legs below the knees, shredding them into strips and entwining them to form a safety line. One end was tied to the hilt of the pole, the other was looped around his wrist. He was taking no chances on losing the net. He doubted whether he had the strength or materials to make another.

He knelt on a corner that jutted out from the rest of the

raft. The fish were there, but catching them was something else again. Fishing took time and patience. He had plenty of both.

Plankton and other single-celled animal life clung to the bottom of the raft. Tiny fish, not much larger, came to feed on them. Bigger fish, still small, fed on them. And so on and so forth, with predators becoming prey on up through the food chain.

Slocum dipped the net into sea. Eased it in, avoiding splashes that would alarm the fish. Its underwater image was blurred, wavery. A chunk of wood was knotted into the bottom of the sack. It tended to rise, helping the sack keep its shape. Slocum played the pole with deft wrist motions, smooth and easy, letting the currents swirl through the net. The sack's lazy drifting movements imitated those of some undersea plant.

At first, the fish shied away from it. After a while, they got used to its presence, accepting it as part of the surroundings. They swarmed under the raft, teeming masses of marine life in all colors of the rainbow.

Slocum let the net trail out toward the rear of the raft. Slowly, steadily, he brought it forward, scooping it up and out of the water.

Seawater sieved through the many pinholes he'd pricked in the sack to keep the liquid weight from bursting it.

What had he caught?—if, indeed, he had caught anything at all.

Hand over hand, he reached up the pole, hauling the still-draining net to him. Suddenly, a fish flipped out of the top. It had yellow and black stripes and was as big as his hand. It arced into the air and down into the water, raising a little splash where it broke the surface.

Cheated, Slocum cried out. The sound of his voice scared him. It was a harsh croak.

Bitterly disappointed, he looked into the sack. A cupful or so of water still remained in the bottom. Thrashing in it was a silver fish, as long as his little finger, but less than half the thickness.

His hand shot out, grasping the sack above the fish so it couldn't escape. He squeezed the water out of the cloth until only the fish remained. He could feel it wriggling.

Slocum closed his fist over the fish in the net. It throbbed like a tiny beating heart. He raised it to his mouth, determined not to lose it, no matter what. That sardine-size fish meant the difference between life and death.

A harsh rasping sound caught his attention. A sound like someone sawing wood. He frowned, puzzled. Then he realized it was the sound of his own panting breath.

He held the netted fish to his mouth and popped it in. It was live, wriggling as he ground it to pieces between his teeth, bones and all. He chewed it to a pulp. A squirt of warm blood trickled down his parched throat. The best brandy in the finest restaurant in New Orleans never tasted one-tenth as sweet.

His throat and mouth were so dry that he could barely swallow. Slow as molasses, the blood trickled down his gullet. The chewed fish pulp was barely a mouthful, but it took him forever to get it down. He nursed it, swallowing a bit at a time.

It was energy—life. His stomach heaved in rebellion, but he kept his rising gorge down. To lose it was death.

It was a help, a start. But he needed much more than that to keep himself alive.

He went back to work. On the next few passes, the pickings were slim. The net yielded no more than a couple of minnows, their combined mass equal to the weight of a copper penny.

He gobbled them down gratefully. Every little bit helped. Each scrap of marine life was transmuted into a fraction of extra life for Slocum. Each drop of fish blood delayed an agonizing death by thirst. Every fleck of meat added energy for his cells to draw on.

The brain-numbing fog of malnutrition lifted slightly, allowing him to play the fish with more cunning. The times that the net came up empty lessened, so that almost every pass yielded some fractional quantity of fish.

It was midafternoon when he first caught a fish as big as his index finger. That was a real prize. He bit off its head and sucked the blood from its body, like a boy sucking sweet syrup from freshly cut sugarcane. His throat was so dry that each swallow brought tears to his eyes.

When he had sucked the last drop of moisture from the fish, he ate it, lingering over every bite. He ate the head, too.

He caught no more than a few morsels until late afternoon, when he made a real strike, netting a fish as big as a roofing shingle. He was terrified that it would escape or that its weight would burst the net. He scooped it out of the water, snatching the top of the net with both hands before it could jump out. It thrashed like a snake in a bag. Gripping it through the fabric, he bashed its brains out against the side of the raft. It twitched like a severed nerve. He held it so tightly that his hands ached. Not until the last tremor had shivered through it, did he release his grip.

It was silver and black banded, and as thick as his hand. Its little puckered mouth was open, revealing rows of sharp teeth. One of its eyes had popped during the bludgeoning. Its underbelly was corpse-white.

It was just about the most beautiful creature Slocum had ever seen.

No part of it went to waste. Its blood was salty, with a

metallic aftertaste. It was the first full mouthful of liquid Slocum had had since early the night before.

He gutted the fish with a sharp stick. He put the bones aside, saving them for later. The meat had a sour, oily taste, but that did not stop him from devouring it. He licked the oil off his fingers. He slit open the stringy guts, washed them clean with seawater, and ate them. He gnawed the thin, membranous tissue from the fins, adding the bones to his collection. Later, he would grind them into powder and eat them.

The single staring eye he saved for dessert.

When he was done, he knew that he had forestalled death for at least another day.

Fish bobbed to the surface where he'd washed out the guts of his catch, drawn by the lingering residue of its juices. Before he could net them, he had to repair the damage inflicted on the net. Some of the strips holding the net to the framework had broken. He retied them, replacing them where necessary.

While making repairs, he took stock of his surroundings. Still no land in sight, no sails on the horizon. During the long day, the raft had drifted to another patch of sea, that was all. That drift might spell doom or salvation.

The ship had gone down off the east coast of the Yucatán peninsula, the coast of the province of Quintana Roo. She'd been sunk somewhere in the Caribbean Sea, south of the island of Cozumel and north of her destination, the port city of Aurora on the Bahia de la Ascension.

The current seemed to be running to the south. Debris from the *Bay* was now spread over a wide band of sea. Slocum was at the mercy of the drift. If it tended toward the southwest, it might carry him to shore, to the coast or to one of the isles that lay off of it. If it ran to the southeast, it would carry him out to sea. If there were crosscurrents, he might remain more or less where he was, drifting until he rotted.

There was always the chance that he might be rescued by a passing ship. It was a slim chance, though.

How many miles was he from land? He didn't know. If he had known, there was nothing he could have done about it, anyway. The raft was too big to steer. He had no control over its movements. He was at the mercy of wind and wave. He could do nothing but try to stay alive as long as possible.

He fixed the net and resumed fishing. The pickings were slim but steady. Bite-size. He didn't eat all he caught. He drank the blood, but some of the meat he saved for later. He stuffed the fish in his pants pockets where they couldn't be swept away.

At sunset, a breeze sprang up. It felt like a breath of heaven. With the sun gone, darkness came quickly.

The night sky was purple-black and star-dusted. Slocum was in no mood to appreciate the view. He searched the horizon for the glow of man-made lights, those of a city or a ship. There was none.

The moon rose. The raft was littered with fish scales, turned silver by moonlight. Slocum made fishing lines. For lines, he used the remaining cloth strips. Bent nails served as hooks. He secured the ends of the lines to the raft and dropped the hooks in the water. For bait, he used a couple of fish scales stuck on the points of the hooks. His paltry store of fish was too precious to waste. He hoped that the fish in the sea would be stupid enough to go for the bright, shiny scales—a scant hope, he had to admit.

Thirst was with him always. He sucked on some of the larger fish bones in a vain attempt to ease it.

The black sea boiled with phosphorescence, the foxfire glow of tiny luminous animalcules without number. If he stared at them for too long they seemed to take on shapes, ghostly elongated forms of wraiths spiraling through the void. He stopped staring. That way led to madness. Many a man in desperate straits might still have survived, had not his reason been unhinged by the pressure of solitude, terrible utter loneliness that made death seem a welcome relief.

The night wore on. Slocum drifted in and out of a troubled half sleep. When the moon was high, he awoke, sick and trembling. His guts were knotted and aching, doubling him with cramps. Something he ate . . .

Spasms of nausea shook him. Fever and chills. He lay curled on his side, hugging himself, riding it out. Moonbeams glided over the waves.

Sometime before dawn, he awoke. He didn't remember falling asleep. He was weak and shaky, but the sickness had passed. He was slick with wetness, moisture that had condensed on him during the night. He used the cloth piece of the fishing net to mop it up, then sucked the wetness from it.

The sun came up and a new day began.

The second day on the sea gave every promise of being a scorcher. It was already hot before the sun came up. That sun could be murderous. Slocum was an outdoorsman. His face was weathered and his torso bronzed. That protected him to some degree from the naked sun, but not enough.

He ate his breakfast, a miserable mouthful of fish that he'd saved from the day before, then he went to work. He pried loose a man-size length of board from the timbers. Placing its midpoint across the raft's upper edge, he leaned his weight against it, breaking it in half. It made a sharp cracking sound, like a pistol shot.

He took the two pieces and wedged them end first into the side of the raft, in the space between two horizontal planks. They stood side by side near the top, jutting out like an awning, which is what they would be: an awning to protect him from the sun's rays. A pair of thinner posts served as uprights to brace the structure. The first stiff breeze to come along might well knock it down, but there was no breeze.

The sun rose, a sullen, smoldering orange disk magnified by haze to twice its normal size. Slocum's head began to throb. He dunked his head covering in cooling water and retied it. It helped a little.

During the morning, he fished. An abundance of marine life swarmed the underside of the raft. What was frustrating was how little of it he netted. He kept at it, slowly amassing a meager catch. Some he saved, some he ate on the spot. It worried him, how little food he took from the sea. Too little to keep a grown man alive for long.

The sun neared its zenith. Slocum told himself that he would knock off soon, after one more catch. The fish weren't cooperating. Suddenly, a tremor rippled through their rainbow-colored ranks.

Fish scattered, fleeing in all directions in a soundless explosion of motion and color. Something had scared them off. *What?*

Splashing nearby made him look up. A fin broke the surface. It was a shark fin.

The beast measured about ten feet long from nose to tail. Its gray-black back was marked with black stripes and dots, identifying it as a tiger shark, one of the most vicious of the species. This one was a particularly large specimen. Slocum was glad that the raft was big and bulky.

The shark was his cue to take a rest. The noonday sun was too brutal to be exposed to, anyway. Slocum sat huddled under his lean-to, hugging his knees.

The sun didn't seem to bother the shark. It circled the

raft, making ever narrower circuits.

Slocum was too sunstruck to care. He watched the shark's movements with dull-eyed apathy.

Some distance away, a few more fins appeared. Their owners clustered together, but they kept their distance from the raft.

All the while, the raft kept drifting, drifting where ... Slocum knew not.

It was getting on toward midafternoon before the sun's heat had declined to the point where Slocum emerged from under the lean-to. He was still sweating profusely, precious moisture that he couldn't afford to lose.

The damned shark was still there. At the closest point of its long, lazy circuits, it approached within ten to twelve feet of the raft. Slocum had developed a healthy respect for sharks after seeing them rip apart and devour the corpses flung overboard from the *Bay*.

Taking up the net, he went to his fishing perch, making every move with care. In his weakened condition, it would be easy to make a misstep and tumble over the side. The tongue of raft extending out into the water seemed smaller and more fragile than he had previously noticed.

The shark neared, sleek, bullet-shaped, and swift. Ugly brute! It came the closest it had yet to the raft, brushing against it. The raft shuddered. Slocum clutched the platform to keep from being thrown off.

The shark wheeled, turning in the water. Its blunt snout headed straight for his perch, making a pass that came within a foot or two of it. It was so close that Slocum could have reached out and grabbed its fin. Its passage made a wave that rolled over the top of the platform.

It came back for a second pass. So far, it seemed interested but not really committed. But who could say what went on in the brain of a shark?

Slocum gripped the pole of the net with both hands. When the shark was within reach, he poked it in the side, hoping to drive it off. The beast seemed to be one solid muscle.

With astonishing speed and violence, the shark struck back. It bent backward so that its head was almost touching its tail. Then it uncoiled, like a bow unstrung, lunging head-first out of the water.

Its underside was as gray as a drowned man's flesh. Black button eyes, bigger than silver dollars, studded the sides of its blunt-tipped snout. Its jaws gaped, baring rows of razor-sharp teeth. Each tooth was the size and shape of a flint arrowhead. Seawater foamed from its maw.

Its jaws snapped shut on the net pole. Slocum snatched his hands away just in time to keep them from being bitten off. Wood crunched, splintering as it was devoured.

The shark fell back into the water with a large splash. Slocum's heart was in his mouth. His wrist burned where the line tethering the net pole had been torn off.

Slocum started cursing. The shark swam away, then doubled back. It wasn't through yet.

It swam toward the raft, moving fast, making straight for Slocum. He jumped, scrabbling to the top. He bumped into the lean-to and knocked it down.

The shark chomped on the end of the raft, the projecting piece from which Slocum had fished. It bit down on the wood and tore it off, a big two-foot section. Worrying it, the shark dove, sinking from sight.

It rocketed upward, out of the water, the tip of its snout reaching halfway up the side of the raft. It thumped heavily against the wood. Its teeth gnashed.

It wants me, thought Slocum.

Its teeth fastened on the end of one of the lean-to's fallen planks. Gravity pulled it back in the water. It took the plank with it.

Water thrashed and boiled around the raft. It shook from a blow from below, as the shark rammed it.

When the shark lunged again, Slocum was ready for it. It leaped. Slocum used the other lean-to plank to whomp it on the nose. He hit so hard that the end of the board broke and flew off.

The shark spasmed. Slocum thrust the jagged end at one of its eyes. The shark flipped backward and swam away.

It didn't go far, breaking surface about midway between the raft and the three sharks clustered a stone's throw away.

Slocum panted, trembling. He shook not from fear but from weakness. The combat had used up much of the little strength he had left.

The net pole was gone. After all the work that had gone into it—!

The thought of making another was too daunting for now. He stretched out across the top of the raft and rested. He kept an eye on the shark. It swam to and fro, not returning to the attack but not going away, either.

Sun and exhaustion worked on Slocum. He drifted in and out of awareness, coming to whenever he thought of the shark.

Once, he let an arm fall, so it dangled down the side of the raft. Tempting bait to dangle before a hungry shark.

That woke him. He glanced where the shark had been, expecting to see it in its now-familiar place.

It wasn't there. It had moved closer, coming at least a third of the distance to the raft.

"You bastard," he croaked.

The shark neither advanced nor retreated. Worse, the other three sharks had come closer.

In the high country, more than once, Slocum's campfire

had been besieged by hungry timber wolves. They prowled at the edge of the light, red eyes gleaming, waiting for his vigilance to flag for the one split second needed to rush in and rip his throat.

Sea wolves. That's what the sharks were. Well, the timber wolves hadn't gotten him and neither would the sharks. All they'd get for their trouble would be the sharp end of a stick in the eye.

6

Women filled the night.

Women. Red, yellow, black, and white. Blonds, brunettes, redheads. Respectable women and whores, sluts and schoolgirls. Young and old, thin and fat. The quick and the dead. Phantom women. Floating in the air above Slocum's head, a legion of them. Their ranks hovered in the cloudy night sky pressing down on the raft. They glowed in the dark, these ladies, a small army of them. The damnedest chorus line Slocum had ever seen.

They were grouped side by side, like a band of paper dolls. Misty outlines, shimmering. Their ranks rippled and billowed stirred by an invisible wind. When they moved, their shining forms blurred and ran together, melting into an eerie aurora.

The wind would stop and the forms would stabilize again. Sometimes, one of the phantoms would emerge from the ranks and descend to Slocum, so close that he could almost reach out and touch her. When he tried, though, she would always float away, out of his grasp. She would rejoin her sisters in the sky. Soon, another would come forth to take her place.

They glowed in the dark and flew in the sky, but they weren't angels, not by a long shot. Slocum knew them, every one. Some were dead and some were alive. Some he hadn't seen for twenty years or more. All appeared as they had been when last he'd seen them.

There was Vangie Pry, the freshest young whore in Abilene during its boom some years back, when the town was the railhead for the big Texas cattle drives. She was the star attraction at the plush Jewel Box House. Ink-black hair spilled down to a wasp waist. Above and below it, her figure ripened into an hourglass shape. High, firm breasts, wide ripe hips.

She was cinched into a skin-tight satin gown, the same one she'd been wearing on that memorable night when the Double Jay and Cross Tee outfits hit town at the same time. The dress was a red so richly seductive it could only be called scarlet. A second skin, the satin shimmered with her every motion, her every breath. It left her shoulders and the tops of her breasts bare. The gown cupped and lifted her already firm breasts, displaying dazzling cleavage. Her nipples were outlined against the material. When she walked, her buttocks rolled, threatening to split the too-tight fabric. She was sleek, provocative, infinitely desirable.

Two men quarreled over her favors, the son of the owner of the Double Jay and the boss of Cross Tee. Back in Texas, the outfits were unfriendly neighbors. There was bad blood between them, but lust for the woman brought out the poison.

Vangie neither encouraged nor discouraged the fight. The men were going to do what they wanted to do, no matter what she said. Why should she stick her neck out?

Tempers flared. The Double Jay scion went for a gun. The Cross Tee foreman shot him down, saving his boss. Drovers for both sides reached and came up smoking.

When the smoke cleared, seven men were dead.

Vangie's eyes were gray. There was no point in taking these idiots seriously. They fought and died because that's what they wanted, more than they wanted a woman. Later, those who lived would want her. The one with the most gold would have her.

Her gaze was serene and untroubled now, too, as she looked down at Slocum. He lay on his back across the top of the raft, looking up. His face was gaunt, strained. His eyes were glazed, rheumy, but he didn't have any trouble seeing her. Why, even with his eyes closed, he could see her clearly.

Vangie Pry. She'd made the mistake of falling in love with the wrong man, a smooth-faced tinhorn. In a jealous rage, she'd knifed him, then hung herself.

Crazy, thought Slocum, *plumb crazy. The jury would have given her a vote of thanks before finding her not guilty for ridding Abilene of that no-account cardsharp.*

Vangie looked good now, as beautiful as she ever was.

Memories, and phantoms of memory, stay forever young.

Got a drink, Vangie? Slocum thought. *I sure could use one. No, not that good red-eye I used to swill back in Abilene. What I crave is a drink of water. I'm dying for one. . . .*

Vangie smiled sadly, fading away. He could see through her to the dark clouds massed behind her. She turned to stardust, scattering to the winds.

The advent of the sharks had spelled the beginning of the end for Slocum. By midafternoon, a school of more than a dozen of them ranged the waters around the raft. Emboldened by numbers, they closed in. The tiger-striped beasts were aggressive, darting under the raft, bumping it, nudging it with their sides.

They couldn't upset it, it was too big for that. They couldn't reach Slocum, huddled on top of it, out of their reach. Teeth gnashed and eyes rolled in fury. Irked, the sharks snapped at each other.

They couldn't kill him all at once, but they were killing him by degrees. He couldn't fish. That meant no food, no water. Once, he got a bite on one of his lines. Improbable as it seemed, a small fish had managed to hang itself up on a bent-nail hook. With infinite care, Slocum lifted the line and began hauling it in, hand over hand, careful to avoid the least little disturbance that might break the fragile hold.

The catch was a scaly, bony fish that had managed to entangle a fin on the line. A slight tremor would dislodge it. Fighting to keep his hands from shaking, Slocum hauled it in.

As the prize neared his gasp, a shark snapped it up and gulped it down. Falling back, the shark raised a splash that wet Slocum's face.

Slocum roared. If he'd had his knife, he'd have gone in after that shark. As it was, he fought down the urge to tackle it with one of the sharp sticks at hand.

The day wore on. Magnified by tension and fatigue, his terrible thirst grew. The sharks prevented him from alleviating it by bathing or even wetting his head covering.

Their frenzy died down, but they didn't go away. There were plenty of smaller fish they could eat while waiting for Slocum. That's what they were doing; waiting, biding their time until he slipped from his perch into the water.

From the way they had devoured the *Bay*'s dead, it would be a ghastly death, but a quick one.

To hell with that. Those smug sea wolves weren't getting him. He wouldn't give them the satisfaction. When the end was near, he'd wedge himself against the timbers and braces in such a way that he'd be jammed in place on top of the raft. Sea birds would peck the flesh from his bones before the sharks would get a bite of it. He'd do it just for spite.

There were seabirds, too, flocks of them. He began noticing them in late afternoon, hordes of screaming white birds racing east across the sky.

Birds couldn't fly around forever. They had to light some time. Did that mean he was near land?

Land lay east, where the birds now flew. They all flew in that direction. At the edge of Slocum's vision, they vanished into a white sky, with no land in sight.

A swell was rising. Waves were higher, their troughs deeper. The ride was getting bumpier.

Slocum was apathetic. It was difficult to maintain a line of thought. He kept drifting away.

Sundown. The drowned sun shot red beams through purple water. Shark fins were black against a copper sky.

Swirling curlicues of hot air corkscrewed in the gloom. A breeze came, became a wind. The sea rose some more.

Daylight closed fast, shoved out by storm clouds. Winds blew. Long, glassy swells rose. Whitecaps crested the waves.

Sea spray splashed Slocum, refreshing him. Thirst, hunger, and exposure had taken their toll. He was weak. His mind drifted, so that his awareness seemed to rise and fall with the restless sea.

From time to time, distant flashes showed. Slocum was unsure whether they were real or imaginary. Finally he decided that they were lightning, striking so far away that all sounds of thunder were lost.

There were lights in the sea, too. At first, Slocum thought they were reflections of the lightning. After studying them, he changed his mind. The underwater lights were brighter and longer-lasting than the flashes.

He lay flat on his belly, head hanging down over one end of the raft, peering into the depths. In a rare moment of lucidity, he realized the hazards of his position. A lunging shark could snag his head between its jaws. He dismissed the thought, arguing that no shark yet had leaped that high. Besides, rough waters had scattered the sharks.

The lights in the sea were fascinating. Green ghost fire danced in coal-black depths. Phosphorescence stirred up by roiling currents.

It shone like city lights, a city in the sea. The more Slocum stared, the more real it seemed. Why, it *was* a city down there, way below the surface!

A sunken city. Not a city of today, like Saint Louis or New Orleans or Houston. This city was old. A walled fortress city, with ramparts and gates and towers, and a central citadel. The only thing Slocum had ever seen like it was in the engraved illustrations in the old family Bible, depicting the ancient cities of the Holy Land.

The city was drowned but not dead. Lights glowed in the windows and the squares, shining with the same foxfire glow as decaying vegetation in a swamp. Through the windows could be glimpsed shapes that might have been the denizens of that watery keep.

Slocum rubbed his eyes but the city remained. Stubborn illusion. Or was it? Perhaps relief, salvation, was at hand. In the city was food, drink, rescue. It would be easy to reach. Dive straight down to it. Why, he needn't even extend himself that much. The water dwellers were sending a conveyance to fetch him. Torpedo-shape, it rose like a rocket, rushing headlong toward the surface.

This vessel had teeth. It was a shark. It went for Slocum. Only the chance timing of the waves saved him. They lifted the raft, taking Slocum beyond the shark's leap.

Sounding like a steel trap slamming shut, the shark's

jaws closed only inches below Slocum's face.

That shook him from his daze. He had no desire to visit the sea bottom in a shark's belly. The sunken city was a phantasm, a delirium dream. He would look on it no more.

He crawled away from the edge, making sure of each handhold. Rising seas buffeted the raft, threatening to shake him loose.

Moving to a safer perch, he carefully avoided looking over the side. So he couldn't have seen the sunken city, still shining in all its ghostly splendor. . . .

When Slocum had first pried up the boards at the top of the raft, he had exposed a long narrow space beneath them, part of the ship's framework. It was seven feet long, two feet wide, and one foot deep: compartment with solid sides and bottom.

Slocum lowered himself into it, feeling like he was climbing into his coffin. It was long enough, but too cramped on the sides. The cramping was good. Wedged in, he would be harder to dislodge. He lay on his back, leaning to one side to make room for his big shoulders. The smell of wet wood was heavy.

The spasm of activity had exhausted him. He watched the clouds massing overhead. Their undersides were lit with intermittent flashes.

He couldn't tell where his skull ended and the night began. Shapes people the dark, taking form: the form of women he had known.

He knew it was delirium, but what of it? They were good company out on the lonesome sea, pleasant illusion. He surrendered to it.

Vangie Pry was the first to separate herself from the sky band and appear to Slocum. As she faded, two little girls took her place.

They were identical twins, about nine or ten years old.

They had long, dark hair and wide, dark eyes. June and Jane Moran, twin sisters Slocum had known in boyhood days, back in the piney woods of his native Georgia.

Lord, he hadn't thought of them in over twenty years! They looked the same as they had the last time he had seen them, right before their family pulled up stakes and headed West. A relative had a prosperous farm in Oregon. The Morans loaded their belongings on a covered wagon and set off on the long trek. They were never seen again. Their people in Oregon tried to trace them to no avail. Somewhere on the trail the Morans vanished into thin air.

The twins were replaced by Lisanne Siebert, a young blond beauty. She wore a white summer dress, decorated with a print design of tiny blue flowers. It clung to her willowy, supple form. A stylish bonnet and a fringed pink parasol completed her outfit. She had worn it that hot July day of the races at the county fair. She was the daughter of one of the richest men in that part of the state. Slocum, just entering his young manhood, had ridden his daddy's prize horse, Starblaze, to victory in a high-stakes race. Lisanne had presented him with the winner's trophy, kissing him on the cheek. Later that summer, during a family sojourn in Mobile, she had caught yellow fever and died.

Lisanne gave way to Mandy Frones. The Froneses were an Ozark hill clan, lawless and wild. Mandy was a true child of the clan. She wore boy's clothes: jeans, boots, and a flannel shirt. Brick-red hair was stuffed inside the crown of a weathered, shapeless hat. But there was nothing shapeless about Mandy. The way her breasts strained the shirt buttons near to bursting showed she was no boy. She had green eyes, pale white skin.

It was in Red River country, a year or two after the war. A gang of Frones plagued the countryside, robbing and killing. They jumped a small cattle outfit that Slocum was riding trail with. The drovers never had a chance. The Frones gang shot them to pieces. Slocum was hit, knocked off his horse. He crawled into the scrub brush near the riverbank.

Mandy found him. Her job was to find the wounded and finish them off. He sat on the ground, leaning back against a tree. Hot sunbeams lanced through the canopy of tall brush overhead. He was hot in the side. The bullet had passed through, but he had lost a lot of blood.

Opposite him, bushes parted, opened by a gun in Mandy's hand. Slocum had lost his gun sometime after he was shot. Mandy eyed him. Whatever she saw must have suited her purposes. She fired a shot into the ground, telling the others that she had shot him.

Later, at night, she came back. She fixed up his wound and give him food and drink. More, she gave him a gun. It was loaded. He raised his eyebrows. "Don't get any ideas," she said.

She had a gun, too. It was drawn and pointed at him.

She wanted to get away from her kinfolk. That was fine with him. They'd run away together. If the Froneses caught her, they'd whip the hide off her, cripple or maybe kill her. Going against the clan was the only unforgivable sin. The guns were for self-defense only.

"Sure, anything you say," Slocum said, straight-faced.

She'd stolen two horses from the gang's remuda. They mounted up and rode all night through the wildest parts of the country, down lost trails only she knew. They rested at dawn in a shady grove carpeted with long, wavy blue-green grass.

He'd recovered enough from his wound to want to grab hold of something live. Mandy was more than willing. In fact, it was part of the package. It was too much trouble to open the buttons of her shirt one by one, so he just tore it open. Her breasts were cream-colored, with wide pink nipples. Her jeans were so tight that taking them down was like skinning a snake. They left red marks on white hips. Her bush was brown with brandy-colored highlights. He tumbled her down on her back in the grass and lay on top of her. His pants were down at his boot tops. When he went into her, she raised her legs, bent at the knees, and hugged his sides with them.

She was a minx. She scored his upper back and shoulders with scratches. He didn't know if she had done it in an excess of passion or because she was a little bitch. Maybe both.

It was too bad that things were the way they were. Slocum wasn't running from the Froneses. He hadn't survived the bloody battles of the war to be spooked by a pack of bushwhacking back-shooters. He took Mandy's gun, in her most unguarded moment. She cussed him up and down for that! He left her tied to a tree, took a horse, and left her the other.

He settled scores with the Frones gang. They'd made camp near water, tending their rustled herd. They were sitting at the fire when Slocum stepped out of nowhere and shot them down; ate their supper, too.

He was mopping the last of the gravy from the tin plate with a piece of bread when Mandy returned. She couldn't have acted warmer or more eager to please, as if nothing could ever make her as happy as seeing her blood kin lying sprawled around the campfire in their own blood.

Slocum knew what she was going to do almost before she did. When she went for the gun of one of the fallen, he shot first. He hated to do it, but there was no choice. If he didn't kill her, she'd keep dogging him until one of them was dead. She was true to the feudist's code and the call of the blood. She died.

"You'd have done the same, Mandy," Slocum said to the apparition.

His words broke the spell, banishing her.

The shades came faster now, parading before his eyes. There was Carlotta Montero, haughty, aristocratic, proud of the royal blood whose lineage she could trace back to Old Spain, to the court of Ferdinand and Isabella. She had been a key player in one of the deadliest range wars in Arizona. She wore a black bolero hat tilted at an angle. Her skin was stretched so taut that the bones of her face showed. Burning eyes and a mouth like a red wound. Hate turned her beauty to something vicious, when she confronted the man who killed her father.

He was a *pistolero,* an assassin. The vaqueros dragged him into the plaza. They'd beaten him pretty badly. He fell to his knees. Carlotta went to work on him with a bullwhip, a thick rawhide blacksnake with a steel tip. It cracked in the air over her head like a pistol report. She laid into the assassin. The lash wrapped around him, slicing through clothes, skin, and the muscles beneath. Bits of flesh flew with each hit.

Before the whipping started, Slocum would have bet that the killer would never rise to his feet again, so brutally had he been beaten. Under the lash, he jumped up, screaming. The vaqueros surrounded him in a ring so he couldn't get away.

Slocum had sold his gun to the Monteros. He didn't take part, but he didn't interfere.

The whip was a fearsome weapon, and Carlotta was a master of it. Each lash tore the skin open to the bone. She could place that steel tip anywhere she wanted with unerring accuracy. A stroke sent the assassin's ear flying. She let him keep his eyes long enough to see his genitals excised by the lash. He collapsed. She kept on flaying him.

When it was clear he had reached the end, the vaqueros sealed him up inside a barrel of vinegar and brine. He was still screaming when they nailed the lid shut, and after, for there was enough air space left to keep him from suffocating.

Next morning, the barrel would be delivered to the assassin's paymaster, as a prelude to the final assault.

There would be killing soon after first light. Slocum decided to turn in early, to be rested for the showdown. He was intercepted on the way to his quarters. Unlike the ordinary hands, who slept in an outbuilding, his gunfighting skills earned him a berth in the big ranch house.

Paco, the foreman, motioned to him. "Come with me, gringo."

When Slocum didn't move, Paco said, "You won't regret it, I promise you that."

Slocum shrugged, went along. The scene earlier had left him restless.

Paco led him to a dark wing of the main house, one Slocum had never been in before. It had been shut up and largely abandoned. Now, candles burned in sconces set along the walls of long corridors. Paco paused at the door of a room. Finger across his lips, he said, "Don't talk, gringo. Don't say anything."

Slocum followed him into the room. Inside were five men, other Montero hands. All were as big or bigger than Slocum, and he wasn't small. They were blank-faced, with glittering eyes. No one spoke. Slocum nodded to the ones he knew, they nodded in return. A couple of bottles of tequila sat on the table. Slocum found an empty seat and sat down. The men smoked and drank, not talking.

After a while, a knock sounded on the door. Paco stuck his head outside and spoke to someone Slocum couldn't see. Paco motioned to one of the men. The chosen one pushed back his chair and he and Paco went out, the door closing behind them.

About twenty minutes later, Paco returned, alone. This time, he gave Slocum the nod. Slocum gulped what was left of his drink and exited.

Paco went down the hall and turned left, Slocum trailing. The branch was dark, but light shone out from under a nearby door. Paco knocked; the door opened from within. He and Slocum entered.

The room was a bedchamber. It smelled musty, as if it had been shut up for a long time. There were other smells, too: sweat, semen, female musk.

Coffee-colored shadows pressed against yellow candle-light in the room. There was an old-fashioned four-poster canopied bed, marble-topped night table and bureau, ward-robe cabinet, a few chairs. A woman was tied to the bed, an old crone hovering by her side.

Carlotta Montero lay spread-eagled on her back. Her arms and wrists were tied to the bedposts. Strong ropes, tight knots. She fought the ropes, twisting against them, marking her skin. A sheet was thrown over her, covering her below the neck. Her hair was undone, hanging loose in tangled disorder. Her eyes were glassy, unseeing. Face taut, mouth open and moaning, making deep guttural cries from the pit of her stomach.

She looked like she was having a fit. She writhed, shaking her hips, arching her back. The sheet fell to her waist. Above, she was bare, with tawny skin and dark brown nipples, neat and pointed. They jiggled as she ground her hips, lifting clenched buttocks off the bed as she thrust her crotch in the air, miming the movements of copulation.

If she knew Slocum or anyone else was in the room, she didn't show it.

The crone at the bedside was an old family servant, a

hunched creature wrapped in black. A black scarf was knotted around her head. Her face was withered like a piece of dried fruit. Her eyes were hard, black.

Atop the night table was a white porcelain basin filled with water. The crone wet a cloth in it, wrung it out, and used it to mop the sweat from her mistress's forehead.

Slocum looked at Paco. Paco said, "The señora gets like this when she's drawn blood."

"How often is that?"

"What do you care, gringo?" Paco was irked.

"I don't. Sorry for asking." Slocum said.

"That's better," Paco said, grudgingly. Voice lower, he confided, "It's the curse of the Monteros, mixing blood and lust. Her father, the padrone—God rest his soul—was the same. Only with him it was women, of course. After a battle, he'd go through five, six of them a night, one after the other. He was a man possessed. After, he could reason again. But not during.

"As is the señora. When the demon is on her, there is nothing for it but to feed her hunger," Paco explained in a low tone.

"I'm starting to get the idea," Slocum whispered.

Carlotta went into a fresh frenzy of writhing and moaning.

The crone mumbled something unintelligible, motioning urgently to the newcomer. A clawlike hand grabbed the sheet and pulled it off Carlotta.

She was naked, with skin like the finest thin-leaf gold. She strained against the ropes, flexing every muscle. Crotch and thighs were moist from the washing the crone had given her between the legs, to freshen her up for the next entrant.

Slocum goggled at her nudity. Impatient, the crone beckoned. Paco put a hand on his back, pushing Slocum forward.

He said, "Gringo, you know what to do."

Slocum shrugged, started forward. He pulled his shirt out of his pants, paused. Nodding toward the crone, he said, "What about her?"

"She stays," Paco said. "If it bothers you, she won't watch."

"The hell she won't," Slocum said.

He took off his shirt, draped it over the back of a chair. Eyeing his torso, the crone nodded approval. She was even more approving when she saw what he had under his pants.

Holding himself, Slocum advanced toward Carlotta. When he reached the bedside, she noticed him. She shivered, licked her lips. She hissed like a snake.

Slocum shuffled doubtfully. "She likes you," Paco said. "Go on, she will not bite."

"Not too hard," Paco added.

Slocum gave him a dirty look as he mounted Carlotta. She growled, shaking her shaggy locks as he entered her. He went deep, changing her growl to a long, drawn-out sigh of voluptuous relief, as if she were sinking into a luxurious, warm bath.

Then she went wild. Fucking her was like going over Niagara Falls in a barrel. She was a tigress, insatiable. Slocum kept on doing it until he couldn't do it anymore.

She used him up and cried for more. He took some comfort in the fact that her cries were weaker than they had been before he'd started. He dressed quickly, on shaky legs.

The crone wet a fresh cloth and washed Carlotta, readying her for the next man. Her eyes had cleared somewhat during the tussle with Slocum, but now that it was done, they were once more glazed, unseeing.

A door to one side of the bed opened on a back corridor.

Paco escorted him out of the room, saying, "You lasted longer than I thought you would."

Paco stood in front of the door, closing it until only a slit of light outlined it.

"This changes nothing," Paco said." Remember that. It never happened. For your own good."

Next morning, at dawn muster, none of the men involved spoke of what had happened. They had other things on their mind, like not getting killed in the upcoming fight.

Carlotta took her place at the head of the troops. She was her usual self, icy and remote, elegantly groomed with not a hair out of place. The Montero crowd rode out, making for the enemy stronghold. Many died in the battle that followed.

Not Carlotta.

Lin Tang was a whore in a house of joy in San Francisco's Chinatown, where Slocum had once wound up in an improbable adventure. She was from Suchow, China. Exquisite, with glossy hair like a plum-black helmet. Amber skin. She wore yellow satin pajamas. Her feet were doll-size, the result of childhood foot binding. Tiny feet were much esteemed by her countrymen, at home and abroad. Many of her clients delighted in nothing so much as being masturbated to climax by the sole of her bare foot.

That was too weird for Slocum. He took her a more direct way. Not necessarily more normal, but direct. He took her from behind, her provocative buttocks wriggling. They wriggled more before he was finished, and so did he.

Lin Tang gave way to Ellen Lane, the worst dancer in the famed Million Dollar Chorus at Johnny Dollar's Golden Palace in Silver City during the boom. As a hoofer, she had two left feet, but she was so beautiful that it didn't matter. There was something endearing about the earnestness of her efforts.

There was Susan London, tall, slim, and utterly lovely, the epitome of Boston breeding and charm. She stood on the patio of the renowned Buckhorn Spa, with a magnificent Colorado mountainscape as a backdrop.

And there was Joyce Fane, the lady gambler who'd broken the bank playing the wheel at Blackie Hawkins's Barbary Coast Club—

Slocum realized what all his phantasmal visitors had in common. They were dead. The twins, Lisanne, Mandy. Carlotta survived the bloody range wars that decimated a county, only to die a few years later from a broken neck in a fall from a horse. Lin Tang burned to death in a fire, trapped along with her brothel mates behind iron gates kept locked by the whoremasters. Susan London succumbed to the consumption that had brought her to the cool, clear air of the mountains in hopes of arresting the disease. Joyce Fane lost her stake to Snake Eyes Barnes one desperate night in Amarillo. There was bad blood between them. Snake Eyes cleaned her out, every cent. She was found dead in her hotel room, a pearl-handled derringer in her hand. It hadn't been fired. She had taken poison instead.

Dead, Slocum thought. *Maybe I'll be dead soon, too.*

Wetness splashed his face. It must have happened more than once to break through to his benumbed awareness.

Even as he took notice, it happened again. And again.

Tears? From his angel band?

Why not? he thought. *Hell, I'm worth it.*

Then: *Bless you, ladies. A little bit longer, now, and I'll be joining you for another round.*

He didn't die, but he got wetter. Droplets pelted him, spattering on contact. Water got into his mouth and nose. Irritated, he rubbed his face, but the drops kept falling.

The ladies were sure crying up a flood. He tasted some of it with his tongue. Fresh, not salty.

Not tears.

Rain.

7

Too much of a good thing can be as bad as not enough. So it was with the rain. Fat droplets pelted Slocum with stinging violence. The clouds opened up and poured, soaking him. Rainwater ran into his open mouth. It rained harder. A half inch of water filled the bottom of the compartment. It sluiced down the sides.

Slocum drank his fill. Sweet water, no salt. He swelled up like a sponge. More rain fell.

The sea heaved, tilted. Waves rose higher than the top of the raft. Slocum got worried. He lay on his side, knees braced, jammed in tightly. He found two good handholds and locked his fists around them.

The raft seesawed, bucking and heaving. If he hadn't been ready for it, Slocum would have been thrown overboard. The wind blew. Rain slanted at a forty-five degree angle. The wind blew harder, till the rain flew almost horizontally.

The big blow came. The raft heeled, almost tipping. For an instant, it stood on its end, hung on the brink, then ponderously righted itself in the trough of the wave.

A wave broke on top of the raft, hammering it with tons

of water. Slocum, who had nearly fallen out on the up-swing, was now smashed into the compartment by the weight of water. Engulfed.

The raft sank, then rose again. Water ran off the top and sides. A wave lifted it above the sea, then dropped it. This happened again and again. There was no particular pattern, no rhythm that Slocum could discern. Sometimes, it was just rising out of the slough when another wave would shove it back down in the deep; other times, the raft rode the wave crests, bobbing on the foam for what seemed like leagues before it was again thrust down.

Slocum held on. When he was underwater, he held his breath, often to the point where his lungs felt like they would burst. More than once, he breathed seawater, only to have it come spewing from nostrils and mouth when the raft finally resurfaced.

Wind shrieked, tearing at Slocum when the raft wallowed above the waves, trying to pry him loose. Waves slammed him, inflicting brutal body blows.

All was howling chaos. Visibility was limited to a few feet in front of his face. There was a sensation of swift, scudding motion as the raft was whipped ahead of the storm.

All sense of duration fled. Slocum reckoned time from one breath to the next. Earlier, when the storm first broke in all its fury, Slocum kept telling himself, *it can't last, not going full-tilt like this.*

It had to blow itself out soon. That's what he thought. Instead, it blew harder, stronger, and longer.

Then he thought, *I can't last.*

He held on, riding out the storm. The battering dashed every thought out of his head. He was an atom of existence, caught in the whirlwind.

The storm slackened. The intervals when the raft was

submerged lessened. Darkness, rain, choppy seas.

There was a noise in the distance, a faint murmuring undertone of unrest. Half deafened by the storm, Slocum was unsure of what he was hearing—if, in truth, he heard anything at all.

But the noise persisted, a hissing growl.

Slocum looked for the source of the sound. For the longest time, nothing. Then, to the leeward, dead ahead, at the very limit of visibility, a line of ragged white fringe divided sky and sea.

Storm whipped the raft straight for the white line. As it neared, growl and hiss loudened.

The white line was breakers crashing against an unseen barrier. Surf. Growling waves, hissing spray.

The raft rushed toward it, eager for destruction. It picked up speed as it neared the breakers. Plumes of spray, as tall as trees, rose where waves crashed against partially submerged rocks.

Now he could see the rocks, black jagged bulks squatting amid the boiling surf.

The wave bearing the raft gathered itself up and swept over the rocks. For a flash, Slocum allowed himself to think that the raft was actually going to make it.

The raft bottomed out on rocky fangs. A shudder ran through it. Beams snapped, boards splintered. The raft ran aground, flinging Slocum from it.

He flew as if shot from a catapult, launched into darkness.

If he hit a rock, he'd smash to jelly. He hit water, sank, currents tossing him this way and that.

He struggled to the surface, splashing, sputtering. He thrashed, fighting panic.

The water wasn't as rough as he'd thought. His feet touched bottom.

Land! He'd been cast ashore—where, he knew not. He struggled up the slope, arms windmilling, feet churning sand.

There was solid ground underfoot, and he was rising from the surf, staggering forward onto an unknown shore.

He was on a wet, sandy beach. Beyond lay a wall of brush.

His legs gave out and collapsed. He fell into a darkness deeper than the blackest night, the darkness within.

Slocum met the investors in a private dining room in the exclusive Maritime Club in Houston. The investors, Pendleton, Deveraux, and Bliss, were titans of industry. Pendleton was a gray-haired, with a silver mustache as sleek and neat as a sable brush. Deveraux, New Orleans banker, heavy-lidded and sallow. Bliss, from East Texas, was burly and open-faced.

They wore dark coats and white shirts. The table was spread with linen and silver, crystal goblets and china plates. Wood-paneled walls. Persian rugs. To one side of the banquet table, an artist's easel held a framed map of Central America, with Yucatán prominently featured.

Bliss wore his hat indoors. Deveraux concentrated on the food, or seemed to. Pendleton did the talking.

He said, "Let's talk business. These gentlemen"—meaning Deveraux and Bliss—"and myself, represent a syndicate of like-minded investors seeking opportunities in Mexico, in the Yucatán. Exporting trade goods and the like."

"Running guns, you mean," Bliss said, snorting. Unlike the others, he drank no wine, only whiskey throughout the meal.

Pendleton glared, but Bliss was unabashed. Bliss said,

"Talk straight, so friend Slocum will know what he's letting himself in for."

Slocum had never met Bliss or the others before this meeting.

Bliss said, "The man's a professional, Pendleton. He wouldn't be here if we didn't know we could trust him."

"No question of that," Pendleton said quickly. "We know you do good work, Mr. Slocum. You come highly recommended."

"Good work"—selling his gun. "Highly recommended"—by other members of the master class who'd hired Slocum with no cause to regret it.

Pendleton rose, going around the table to the map. He used a butter knife for a pointer, indicating a point on Yucatán's east coast.

He said, "South of the island of Cozumel, on the mainland, is the Bay of Ascension, an anchorage big enough to shelter an entire fleet. And here, on the bay, is the port of Ciudad Aurora. A certain faction of highly placed individuals among the city's rulers has contracted with our agent for a consignment of munitions."

"Smuggled cargo," Bliss said, "guns and bombs."

Pendleton watched Slocum for his reaction. Slocum shrugged, said, "Business is business."

"Just so," Pendleton agreed, nodding briskly.

Bliss drank more whiskey. Deveraux, silent throughout, nibbled a piece of his entrée like a chicken pecking a grain of corn.

Pendleton said, "Referring to the cargo as *smuggled* rather overstates the case. *Contraband* is a more accurate word. A mere technicality, due to the fact that it would be politic for the transaction to escape the official notice of the Mexican government."

He smiled thinly. "Unofficially, I can assure you that the

Mexicans intend to maintain a laissez-faire attitude.''

Bliss said, ''That means they've been bribed to look the other way.''

Bliss was red-faced, perhaps from the whiskey. Sweat shone on his jowls, grease smeared his mouth. He shoveled forkful after forkful of food into his mouth.

Slocum said, ''What do you need me for?''

''To ride shotgun on the guns,'' Bliss said, through a mouthful of food.

Pendleton sketched out the plan. The weapons were cached in a ship, which would remain nameless unless and until Slocum took the job. The secret of the guns was unknown to the crew, except for the skipper. Slocum would book passage to Aurora on the ship. He would make sure the guns reached their rightful claimants, guarding against treachery by any and all interested parties. His role as the investors' agent would be unknown to the skipper.

There were more embellishments, but that was the gist of it. Slocum opened the money talk, inviting the others to name a figure. Pendleton did so. Slocum named his figure.

Pendleton winced, Bliss choked, and Deveraux made a grimace of distaste.

Through a haze of brandy fumes and cigar smoke, the dickering went back and forth. Suddenly, Slocum was seized with a sense of déjà vu, as if he'd already lived this scene before.

A curious split took place. The scene progressed, with Slocum playing out his part; yet another corner of his mind, detached from all the rest, watched the performance, knowing what was to come but unable to affect the outcome.

No! cried the silent observer. *Don't do it!*

''I'll do it,'' Slocum said, ''now that we've come to terms.''

''Splendid!'' said Pendleton.

The deal was closed. They drank on it, Slocum and the investors. Slocum tossed back his, Bliss did the same, Pendleton took a swallow, and Deveraux, a sip.

Pendleton set down his glass, barely touched. "Now that you're on board, so to speak, ha ha, you may as well know the name of the ship. She's the *Matagorda Bay,* Captain Hoyt, skipper."

Too late! Too late!

"Never took a sea cruise before," Slocum said. "Sounds kind of restful."

The investors were silent, stiff-faced, unmoving. Color fled from their skin. They looked like waxworks dummies.

Something poked Slocum in the side.

"Ow," he said.

He looked around to see who'd done it. Not the investors. They were beyond reach, in more ways than one.

Another poke, a sharp prod on the shoulder. Slocum bristled, but his assailant remained unseen.

An invisible hand seized him by the arm and shook him.

All at once, Slocum took notice of himself. Something was different from his recollection of the meeting in Houston. The first time, he'd been dressed in a manner befitting dinner at a businessmen's private club.

Now, he was naked, except for a pair of tattered, cut-off jeans. He was filthy, sun-blasted, and starved, exhibiting the effects of extreme exposure and privation.

He chuckled.

Imagine showing up for a big meeting looking like a shipwrecked castaway! That's one on me—them, too!

Investors, private dining room, all faded away, like smoke blown by wind.

Slocum lay facedown in the sand, arms pillowing his head. Sunlight was hot on his back.

Investors, Houston, all a dream, a memory of the events

leading to his passage on the *Bay* and all that followed.

The shaking, the poking and prodding, remained. Real enough to have shaken him awake from his remembered dreamworld.

He raised his face from the ground and looked up. A ring of natives surrounded him, about two dozen or so, mostly males. Some females stood at the outskirts, craning for a better look.

Slocum guessed they were Indians, Yucatecan Indians of a type unfamiliar to him. A handsome folk, with thick, straight black hair, dark almond-shaped eyes, amber skin. The tallest was not much more than a few inches over five and a half feet tall; most of the others were less. They were straight, supple, slight. The males wore a woven loincloth, the females a thin white shift.

A male squatted beside Slocum, roughly shaking him. He jumped to his feet, startled, when Slocum stirred. The others recoiled, then advanced, muttering darkly.

They seemed unfriendly at best. Those in the front line were armed with stone-tipped spears, clubs, knives, machetes. Even a few rifles, old flintlock muskets, were aimed at the castaway.

Slocum was now a captive of the Maya.

8

Long before Christ, the Maya were kings of the forest. In the mountains and jungles of the Yucatán, they raised great cities of pyramids, plazas, and palaces. Priests kept the sacred calendar, calculating an astonishingly accurate 365-day year. Kings and conquerors connived at empire. Dynasties rose and fell, city-states grew and died. And always, the jungle lurked at the outskirts, pressing the edges, ceaselessly seeking to reclaim the settlements that had been wrested from it.

When the conquistadores arrived with their Spanish galleons, horses, armor, and firearms, they truly were men from another world. Being men, they sought plunder, conquest, empire. Not force of arms, but culture shock slew the great Maya civilization, as it did that of the Aztecs to the north. Cities fell. Thousands were slaughtered. More died of newly introduced Old World diseases, for which they lacked all natural immunity. Survivors were enslaved to toil in the fields of their new lords. Jungle quickly covered the deserted cities, hiding them as thoroughly as if they had never been.

Many Maya fled to the mountains and swamps to escape

the conquerors. Long after the Aztecs and the Inca of Peru had ceased to resist, the Maya kept the struggle alive, fighting fierce battles against the Spaniards. Yucatán's east coast, the coast of Quintana Roo, was never totally subjugated. In 1850, the mystic Talking Cross triggered a full-scale Maya revolt against the European invaders. This War of the Castes delivered a full measure of horror, with atrocities and massacres on both sides. It did not so much end as peter out from exhaustion.

Now, more than three decades later, it was still worth the life of a *vecino,* a white, to be caught outside the cities of Quintana Roo. Such was the custom of the free Maya.

The captive, the man from the sea, was no *ladino,* but he was unquestionably white. Tradition with the force of law decreed his death. Yet this was no ordinary man, for he had been cast up on these shores by the sea.

These matters were carefully considered by Yax Balam, chief of the tribe that had found the stranger. He numbered more gray hairs than black, but his strength and cunning were undiminished.

The tribe's fortunes had fallen under an evil star. They were fisher folk barred now from the rich fishing grounds. The cause was no mystery. Others of the cursed whites had profaned the sacred shrine of Tlaloc, the Rain God, master of all the watery element in this world and the other. In revenge, Tlaloc had sent a Sea Beast, one of his sacred monsters, to afflict the tribe until the wrong was righted.

Why the deity had chosen to punish the tribe rather than the profaners was a mystery that did not readily reveal itself to mortal mind.

And now, the man from the sea had appeared. Best not to deal with him too hastily. He was the sea's whose gods might resent any ill use he received. Perhaps his arrival at this crucial hour was a godsend, a sign of deliverance. Perhaps not.

The gods would make their will known. Until then, the stranger would live.

So ruled the headman, Yax Balam.

Slocum was too weak to walk. The Maya carried him off on a litter. It took six men to carry the load. Others went forward and behind, in a state of grim excitement.

The procession climbed to the top of a low ridge overlooking the beach. The sandy strip curved in a long horseshoe shape, with capes at the north and south forming the arms. Lying offshore, not far from the points, lay the arc of a chain of coral reefs, many half submerged. This was the barrier against which the waves broke. It turned the horseshoe bay into a lagoon, with relatively peaceful, shallow waters.

Grounded on a reef was a hulking mound of driftwood, the remains of the raft. The crash last night had thrown Slocum into the lagoon, from which he had struggled ashore.

The litter was made of two planks laid lengthwise, with three supporting cross-poles beneath. The ends of the poles were gripped by bearers, three per side. The wood had been salvaged from the raft.

Slocum rose off his back, up on his elbows for a better view. A lonely shore, inhabited solely by Maya. The landscape gave no clue as to whether he had landed on an island or the mainland. Either way, he had a feeling he was a long way off from Ciudad Aurora.

Low, flat-topped, the ridge ran parallel to the shore. A hundred yards inland, the brush began. The ground between was rocky. A footpath stretched across it, closer to the edge of the ridge than the bush.

Litter-bearers and guards marched north, churning up clouds of gray-white dust. What Slocum saw of the interior of the country was uninviting: endless low hills, matted with thick scrub brush. Parched, thorny, forbidding. Last night's deluge had done little to ease this thirsty land.

Cloudless sky, brazen sun. Birds perched on the twisted limbs of leafless trees, exhausted by the heat.

After a quarter mile, the ridge ended, sloping gently down to the beach. The shoreline cut inward to form a sheltered cove. The cove was beyond the lagoon, facing the open sea, but some lesser reefs broke the waves main force a good distance from shore.

On the opposite side of the cove, the ridge began again. On top of it was a stone tower, a watchtower, very old.

At the inner edge of the beach, a long, shallow hill rose to a series of mounds with broad flat tops and slanted sides. They were overgrown with vines and creepers, but their unique size and shape so differed from the surrounding landforms that it seemed safe to say they were man-made. They were clustered in the northeast corner of the cove.

Behind them were cliffs, rising to a plateau a hundred feet above sea level. There was a gap in the wall, the mouth of a valley that fanned out into the interior. A stream ran down the valley, through the cove, and into the sea.

Overlooking the pass was a loaf-shaped mound. Atop it was a group of thatched huts, the village.

The procession angled across the hard gray sand toward the village. Grit crunched beneath the sandaled feet of the litter bearers. Their martial tread echoed in the bowl-shaped cove.

At the end of the beach, a path sloped across stony fields to the mounds. At one point, it crossed the creek. Spanning the gap was a stone bridge of incredible antiquity. Its decorative carvings were worn away, weathered by centuries.

The marchers crossed the bridge. Ahead, tribespeople thronged the village, eager to see the prodigy. Some climbed down the sides of the mound for a better view.

Nearing the mound, Slocum saw that his first guess was correct: it *was* artificial. One of its short sides fronted the pass, its long sides paralleled the shore. Stonework, masonry showed where its thick dirt crust had worn away.

Rounding the corner, the marchers made for a wide stone stairway in the middle of the mound's east face. From this angle, other mounds could be seen, rising in terraces. They were all even more overgrown than the first, indistinguishable from natural hills to those unaware of their secret.

The mound complex must have been a city of some sort. Slocum had encountered pre-Columbian artifacts before: the deserted Southwest canyon cities of the Anasazi, the Old Ones; enigmatic giant rock carvings on the cliffs of the Colorado River; the pyramids of Teotihuacan in the Valley of Mexico. That great lost cities were buried in the Yucatán jungle had been made known to the English-speaking world as far back as the 1840s, reported by traveler John Stephens.

Slocum wondered how long it took for the mound complex to reach its present state of ruin. Two, three hundred years? Five hundred? More?

The question was academic, but it gave him something to think about besides his lack of a plan for escaping the Indians. Even if he'd had one, he lacked the strength to carry it out.

All he could do now was drift with the tide, something he'd had plenty of practice at lately.

At least he was on dry land. If he never went to sea again, it would be too soon.

The litter bearers made the long climb to the top of the

mound. Slocum couldn't have made it under his own power.

The mound top was covered with dirt. A dozen huts were grouped around an oval central space. Mayans filled the plaza. Men, women, children, about eighty in all. They moved aside as the stranger came among them.

They were quiet, not friendly, but not openly hostile. That meant nothing. A man's face doesn't always mirror his intentions. Slocum knew that torture of captives was fairly widespread among the warlike tribes of the plains and the desert. There was no reason to believe that the custom hadn't reached the Yucatán. If his captors were so inclined, the torture wouldn't start right away. In his current condition, he was too weak to put on a good show. They'd wait until he was strong enough to bear up under the treatment for a while.

If that was the case, then an opportunity to escape might present itself before the appointed hour. It had damn well better, Slocum told himself. If not, he'd just have to make that opportunity happen.

The huts had cylindrical shapes with mushroom-shaped roofs. They were made of thatching on wooden pole frameworks. The bases were raised a foot off the ground.

The bearers carried him into an empty hut. In the center of the floor was a hole lined with stones for a cooking fire. There was a hole in the roof to let the smoke out. Woven hammocks were strung from upright wooden pillars.

The bearers unloaded Slocum from the litter to a hammock, then exited. A warrior stood guard over him; two more were posted outside the door of the hut.

The hammock was surprisingly comfortable—more so than the plank litter, anyway. Ropes creaking, it swayed gently, lulling him.

The guard was silent, stone-faced. He stared steadily at

a point in the hut where Slocum was not.

A scuttling sound caught Slocum's lazy interest. Tethered to a stake in the dirt floor by a long cord around its neck was an iguana, a sea-green reptile with goggling gold black eyes. "You and me both, friend," Slocum said. The iguana gulped down a bug.

As the afternoon wore on, Yax Balam took counsel with the other powers of the tribe. He was *ahau,* a lord of noble blood. That made him *cacique,* but his power as chief was not absolute. Other factions had to be reckoned with.

Tata, the elder, was shaman, high priest, the intermediary between men and gods. Lady Xoc, also *ahau*, was a witch of ill repute. Tzotzil was foremost among the warriors.

The foursome met apart from the others in a shady spot outside the ring of huts on the mound.

Yax Balam said, "Now, what of this man from the sea?"

"Kill him," Tzotzil said. "Say the word, and I'll kill him myself."

His hand went to the hilt of his knife, a glassy black dagger wrought from a chunk of volcanic obsidian from distant highlands.

Tata cluck-clucked. He was old, white haired in a harsh land where few could count on living long enough to see their first gray hairs. Poking out from under the snowy mane was a bleary-eyed tortoise face. His flesh was withered, with sagging dugs like an old woman.

Wagging a finger at Tzotzil, he said, "As ever, you are too quick to slay."

The warrior's face set in hard lines. "No white man may set eyes on us and live."

He looked to the woman for support. "Is that not so, my lady?"

Lady Xoc, beautiful, childlike, deadly. She answered

Tzotzil with a gesture signifying neither approval nor assent, but merely that she had noted his comment.

Tzotzil, surprised, said, "Death to intruders, is not that the law of the Maya? And the Cruzob?"

At mention of the latter, Lady Xoc frowned. "You forget yourself, warrior. It's not for you to speak to me of such things."

Tzotzil knew that he'd gone too far. "Forgive me, my lady."

The Cruzob were the followers of the Talking Cross, the mystic relic that had sparked the War of the Castes and kept the Yucatán in ferment for the last thirty years or so. They killed any whites they caught. The movement was especially strong in Quintana Roo. Lady Xoc was well connected to Cruzob ruling circles. The Cruzob were potent friends and lethal foes. Should he run afoul of them, Tzotzil was doomed.

Lady Xoc was mindful to be merciful to the warrior, this time at least. She nodded.

"You but spoke with a warrior's bold heart," she said.

Tzotzil, ever the stoic, managed to hide his relief.

"Yet this is no simple matter of swift death," she added. "An intruder may be slain out of hand, yes, but not the man from the sea."

"That is so," Yax Balam said, speaking for the first time since the meeting's start.

Tzotzil's outrage bubbled up. "How is this? Not kill him?"

The lady's laugh was bright, silvery. "Of this be certain, warrior: the man must die."

Tzotzil backed off, pleased. He had gotten what he'd wanted.

The old shaman, Tata spoke.

"These are evil times," he said, shaking his head. "The

rains do not come. Our corn withers in the fields. And the
Sea Beast bars us from our hereditary fishing grounds, the
ocean harvest that is our birthright and our very life.''

"Blessed though the beast be," he added piously, not
wanting to incur the monster's wrath.

Yax Balam said, "Perhaps the gods have sent us the
stranger as a sign that their divine displeasure is ended."

"As an offering," Lady Xoc said.

Tzotzil nodded. Tata smacked his toothless gums. Yax
Balam, thoughtful, pursed his lips.

He said, "This is too dark for human understanding. We
must seek counsel of the Vision Serpent."

Slocum slept fitfully and awoke feeling more tired than
he'd been before he started.

Three females entered the hut, framed by a portal filled
with golden sunset light.

Slocum was not so far gone as to fail to notice that all
three were damned attractive.

Two carried food and drink; behind and apart from them
stood the third. She was in command, deferred to by the
others, including the guards. She communicated with a nod,
a glance, a subtle gesture.

She motioned to the female attendants, who went to Slocum. Bracing his feet on the floor, he sat up in the hammock.

A guard started forward, only to be checked by a word
from the lady. He fell back, arms crossed on his chest,
squinting suspiciously at Slocum.

The serving girls wore their long, dark hair down to the
waist. Finely molded features, downcast eyes. Sleeveless
white shifts decorated with colorful embroidery reached
down to their knees. Backlit by sunset, their forms could
be seen through the thin fabric. They were worth seeing.

Their names were Chicha and Naabi, for so the lady addressed them. Unrolling a woven mat, they placed it on the floor beside the hammock. On it they set out the gourds and clay pots containing the meal. There was water, coconut milk, fruit, tortillas, and dried fish.

Slocum ate and drank. If they wanted to kill him, they wouldn't use poison. He had a little of everything except the dried fish. His stomach wasn't up to that challenge yet.

When he was done, he lay back in the hammock. The girls cleared, withdrawing to the far side of the hut, where shadows grew.

Now the lady stepped forward. Marks of high status showed in her attitude, garb, and ornaments. Little more than five feet tall, her height was magnified by an ornate hairstyle. Waist-length tresses were bound up at the top of her head, the whole intricate arrangement held in place by handsome tortoiseshell pins. She carried herself with an air of assurance foreign to the serving girls—or the guards, for that matter. A beauty, strong-willed and willful. Her white garment was the most elaborately embroidered of the three. She was adorned with long jade earrings, a necklace strung with bits of jade and coral, and dozens of wire-thin silver bracelets.

Looking down at him, she said, "How are you called, O man?"

She spoke in Spanish, good Spanish, better than his. All he'd heard up to now since making landfall was Mayan, whose every word was a mystery to him. He was so surprised, he forgot to reply.

She repeated the question. He told her his name.

"Sloh Koom," she said.

Close enough.

"I am Lady Xoc," she said, pronouncing it the Latin way, with the X standing for the SH sound: Lady Shock.

She said, "How came you hence, Sloh Koom?"

"Shipwreck."

She leaned forward, studying him. Her face caught the full force of the golden light, accenting a network of fine lines around her eyes and mouth.

Slocum realized that she was not in her teens, like Chicha and Naabi, but was at least ten years older. A mature woman, with the face and figure of a seductive young girl. A most unusual woman, to retain the bloom of youth at an age when most of her peers had faded from the rigors of multiple childbirth, endless toil, and exposure to sun and sea.

Dangerous woman.

She said, "You are not *ladino*."

"No, *norteamericano*."

"A gringo."

"Yes."

Her smile failed to reach her eyes. She said, "When I lived at the mission school, there was much talk of the gringos, about how they wanted to steal all Mexico."

"Don't believe everything you hear."

"No?"

"No," he said. "Why, we aim to steal the world before we're done."

"That I believe," she said.

"Mission school? That's where you learned to speak Spanish?"

"Yes."

"You speak it well."

"Thank you."

"Where am I?"

"Don't you know?"

"No."

"You have fallen among the People of the Sea, Sloh Koom."

He wanted to ask how near, or far, he was from Ciudad Aurora, but caution kept him from volunteering information about himself or his destination.

He said, "What's the nearest town?"

"Why, don't you like it here?"

"The company is charming, but my people will be worried about me," he said.

The only people who'd be worried about him were Pendleton, Deveraux, and Bliss. When they learned the fate of their arms shipment, they'd happily consign him to the depths along with their contraband.

Lady Xoc said, "You must allow us to show you our hospitality, Sloh Koom. It may surprise you."

That could be taken a lot of ways, not all of them good.

She said, "We have talked enough. You are tired. Rest now."

The interview was at an end. Lady Xoc exited, with Chicha and Naabi in tow. Slocum was alone with the guard and the iguana.

Clawed feet skittered in the dirt as the reptile strained at the end of its tether, struggling to get free. A black beetle scuttled past at a tangent. The reptile abandoned the struggle and ate the bug.

Slocum said, "Hmmm."

This is the world of flesh; the domain of spirit is the Otherworld. The gods live in the Otherworld. They act in this world through signs, portents, and mysteries. Such a mystery was the advent of the Man from the Sea.

The food of the gods is blood. To give the gods flesh in this world, it is necessary to spill blood. This is why the

Aztecs and the Maya practiced ritual bloodletting and mass human sacrifice.

By letting blood, the leader unites the tribe with the gods. If the ritual is a success, Vision Serpent reveals the will of the gods to the seeker.

When the moon rose, Yax Balam invoked the gods.

Guards remained behind in the village. The rest of the tribe gathered at the foot of the stone tower on the ridge to witness the ritual.

The four-sided tower had a flat roof. Flights of stairs angled up to it. Standing on the platform was the chief, two attendants, shaman Tata, and Lady Xoc. They faced east, outlined by the moon shining over the sea. The surf beat. Torches fluttered in the breeze.

Set on an altar were sacred objects: a bowl, strips of white cloth, obsidian knives, and stingray spines.

Tata conducted the lengthy preritual ceremonials. He wheezed on, tireless as a bellows. A small band of musicians played flutes and drums. The pipes shrilled in the bones of the skull, the drums vibrated in the pit of the stomach. The tribe gave themselves up to the rhythm.

Tata chanted the call, the tribe chanted the response. The music droned. The effect was hypnotic.

High priest, chief, musicians, worshipers, all swayed as one.

Revelation was at hand. Yax Balam, glassy-eyed, signaled for the knife. One was put into his hand by an attendant. The blade of volcanic glass was razor-sharp.

The chief slashed the inside of his forearm, drawing blood.

Lady Xoc shivered voluptuously, hugging herself.

The chief cut himself some more, on both arms. An attendant held the bowl under the wounds, collecting blood.

This was only the prelude.

The knife was put aside and the perforators taken up. Stingray spines, barbed quills about a foot long.

Yax Balam gripped his lower lip firmly between thumb and forefinger and pulled it out, away from his mouth. He pierced it with a stingray spine, pushing it halfway through and leaving it there. A second quill pierced his upper lip.

A third pierced his tongue.

More blood for the bowl, much more.

Pipes piped, drums drummed. Power charged the night. The moon shone bright as a god's face.

Shuffling stiff-legged, entranced, the chief fumbled with his knotted loincloth. He took it off, exposing his nakedness.

Bats flapped out of tarry black woods, skittering across the sky.

Yax Balam pinched together a fold of skin on his penis and pierced it with a sharpened quill.

The ritual neared its peak. The bowl was held beneath the chief's member while he withdrew the quill.

Bowl of blood. The level rose.

Strips of cloth were wrapped around his member. Quills were removed from lips and tongue.

Yax Balam stumbled on through the dance, swaying, circling. The attendants guarded against his falling off the platform.

In an ecstatic trance, the chief felt his soul take wing. Roaring sounded. A vortex opened and swallowed him.

He collapsed. He lay twitching on the platform, sightless eyes open. When the spasm finally passed, he sat up, rubbing his eyes.

"Vision Serpent has told me what to do," he said.

Tata displayed the bowl of blood to the people, that they might see that the ritual had been done in the proper way.

The tribe cheered.

9

The reptile didn't like Lady Xoc. When she came to the hut to visit Slocum, the iguana went the other way, getting as far away from her as the tether allowed. It only had that reaction in her presence. It was more or less oblivious when others entered, such as the serving girls or the guards. The phenomenon intrigued Slocum. There must be something mighty unusual about the lady to have that effect on a cold-blooded reptile.

The iguana was an ugly cuss, but Slocum had developed a sneaking fondness for it. It left him alone and ate a lot of bugs that otherwise would have infested the hut.

Slocum paid more attention to his surroundings now that he was on the mend. He was mostly rawhide, leather, and bone: hard to kill and quick to heal.

For two days, he ate and slept. On the third day, he was ready to get back on his feet.

He was fed twice a day, at morning and evening. On the morning of the third day, Chicha and Naabi brought his food, according to the usual routine. Sometimes Lady Xoc accompanied them, sometimes not. True to her title of nobility, she never carried out the menial tasks of serving and

110

cleaning, leaving them to the girls. Later, when they were done, she would visit with Slocum. Many of her questions had to do with politics, such as the position of the Mexican and United States governments to the secessionist movement in Yucatán. Slocum didn't have to pretend ignorance on the subject, but he allowed that, considering how things had worked out for the Confederate States of America, secession might not be the best way to go. Privately, he guessed that the smuggled arms shipment might well have been destined for the secessionists in Aurora, a hunch that might or might not prove useful at a later date.

After his morning meal on the third day, Slocum communicated to the serving girls that he wanted to see their mistress by repeating the word "Xoc" until they got the idea.

As they crossed to the exit, Slocum admired the roll and sway of their sassy buttocks under their *huipils,* as the white one-piece dresses were called. Chicha, slimmer, had a pert rounded rump. Naabi's backside was ripe, full.

As they went out through the portal of the hut, they looked back over their shoulders and caught Slocum eyeing them. Naabi humphed, sticking her nose in the air. Chicha gave him a long, calculating look.

When they were outside, they started giggling.

A quarter-hour passed. Slocum, restless, paced around the hut. The iguana ignored him. The big gringo and the reptile had the hut to themselves, no guard having been posted inside since the second day.

Two guards stood outside the hut, however, and they were armed with knives and machetes. They didn't like it when he stuck his head outside. They stepped back—not from fear, but to leave space for them to draw their machetes if he rushed them. Their hands were on the hilts of their weapons.

A guard spoke with a rush of words, motioning for Slocum to go back inside. Slocum played the fool, making like he didn't get the message. He took a quick survey of what he could see from the doorway of the hut.

Summoned by the loud words of the door guard, more guards came. They had been lurking nearby, just out of sight. Two two-man teams closed in from different directions. Each team included one member armed with a long rifle, and one bowman with a quiver of arrows.

The muskets were leveled at Slocum. Arrows were notched in the bows, whose strings were held ready to be drawn, if necessary. The door guards moved off to the sides, opening a clear field of fire.

Nodding and smiling, Slocum stepped back into the hut.

The two-man teams drifted away, leaving the door guards in place. Slocum sat in the middle of the hammock, feet on the floor.

"Well, I know where I stand," he said.

He was under no illusions. Those old-time muzzle loaders were antiques compared to today's lever-action Winchesters, but they could still blow a hell of a big hole out of their target. Their wielders looked like they knew how to use them, too.

Those arrows were no joke, either. Three feet long, with wickedly barbed heads.

The reptile whipped its head to the left, goggled, blinked; whipped its head to the right, goggled, blinked; faced front, thrust its head forward on the end of its neck, blinked, retracted it, and lay down.

Time passed. Slocum rose and went to the side of the hut opposite the entrance. The guards weren't watching him. He turned his attention to the wall. It wasn't much, just dried leaves and branches set in a stick framework. He could knock it down without half trying.

Daylight showed through tiny gaps in the thatching. Slocum stuck his fingers in one of the gaps, widening it. When the hole was wide enough to see through, he put his eye to it.

Staring back at him was the black bore of a musket. He pulled his head back in time to keep from being poked in the eye.

The sentry standing on the other side of the wall thrust the rifle barrel a few inches inside the hut. Slocum went back to the hammock.

With a rustle of dead leaves, the weapon was withdrawn.

Soon after, Lady Xoc arrived. A guard started to follow her into the hut. She waved him away, and he withdrew.

The reptile darted across the floor, scuttling as far from her as it could get before being jerked short at the end of its tether. It crouched low into the dirt and lay there, panting.

Lady Xoc said, "You are restless today, Sloh Koom."

"I wanted to take a walk, but the guards didn't like it."

"They only want to protect you."

"They've got a funny way of showing it," he said. "Protect me from who?"

"You are a great curiosity to my people, O man from the sea. The guards shield your privacy from idle gawkers."

"I'm the sociable type. I like to get out and meet the folks."

"How very American of you! If you like, I can show you something of our village and island."

Island, Slocum noted. It was the first hard fact he'd learned about his present whereabouts.

"I'd like that," he said.

At midmorning, the excursion began. Lady Xoc and Slocum walked side by side. Chicha and Naabi followed a few paces behind their mistress. Bringing up the rear, about a dozen paces behind, was an armed escort of four warriors, equipped with muskets, machetes, and knives.

It was hot, but still cool compared to what it would be a few hours later, when the sun was high. Many people were in the village, grouped around their huts, attending to various chores. They eyed Slocum and his entourage with blank-faced indifference—whether real, or a mask to hide their true feelings, Slocum could not say.

North of the village rose a second, higher mound. Its top was littered with stone pillars, some still standing. In its heyday, it must have been a temple or great hall.

And how long ago was that? Not even Lady Xoc knew.

"When my people first came here, generations ago, the ruins were already there," she said.

A footpath wound through the bush at the base of the temple. Through gaps in the woods the sea could be seen.

Screaming erupted high overhead, giving Slocum a start. The source was a black-faced howler monkey, perched in the top bough of a tree. Its shriek was disturbingly human.

The howler broke off twigs and threw them at Slocum. A shot boomed. The monkey was hit, blown off its perch. It fell through the branches, landing with a thud near the base of the tree.

Monkeys in other trees shrieked in chorus.

The shot had come from one of the armed escort, the haughty warrior Tzotzil. Smoke rose from the barrel of his musket as he handed it to one of his men, replacing it with a loaded weapon. Sneering, he shook the gun in defiance.

The warrior who'd surrendered his gun retrieved the monkey, lifting it by the tail and dropping it into a game basket. He lingered behind to reload, racing to catch up with the others who'd already gone on ahead.

The path spilled out of the woods onto the north ridge

overlooking the sea. Emerald waters glinted with dazzling highlights where the sun struck the waves. A sentry stood atop the stone tower, facing south.

Slocum said, "Must be some view from up there."

"Would you like to see it?" Lady Xoc said.

"Yes."

The lady and he climbed the stairs, she leading. The tower was made of stone blocks fitted together with mathematical precision. As far as Slocum could tell, no mortar was used on the masonry.

The stairs angled up the sides of the tower. Lady Xoc rounded the corner at the top of the first flight. Slocum glanced at the others on the ground. Tzotzil sneered up at him. Slocum had him marked down as trouble.

When he reached the top, Slocum was winded. He was far from recovered from his ordeal, but he could feel himself coming back.

Lady Xoc spoke a few words to the lookout. He bobbed his head in a bow and withdrew to the stairs so she and Slocum had the platform to themselves.

The tower was the highest point on the island. Looking west, over the treetops, Slocum saw a hazy green arc that must be the coast of the mainland.

North, south, east, and west, the only sign of human habitation was the Mayan village.

Surf broke on the offshore reefs. Slocum looked for his raft but couldn't find it. It had been salvaged, Lady Xoc explained, both for its useful driftwood and for its infinitely more valuable commodity, metal nails. There was no ore on the island, and what metal the People of the Sea possessed, they had acquired with great difficulty.

A fair wind blew, but only a few boats had put out to sea. Most of the boats were beached. Strange behavior for fisher folk, thought Slocum.

Lady Xoc pointed out a distant rock to the south, hovering at the edge of visibility.

"That is Scorpion Island," she said, using the Spanish, Isla Alacran.

Waiting for his reaction, she got only polite interest.

"Scorpion Island, that means nothing to you?" she pressed.

"No. Should it?"

"If it does not, then it should not. A good place to avoid, fit only for scorpions and other crawling things," she said.

She changed the subject, but Slocum wasn't so quick to put it out of his mind. She'd been fishing for something she hadn't found, but the island held a special significance for her. Too bad he couldn't place it. It might have helped him orient himself on the map. Scorpion Island.

Yellow-white heat waves shimmered on the jade sea. Time for Slocum to get out of the sun. He and Lady Xoc prepared to quit the tower.

The sentinel returned to the platform, holding a cabbage-size conch shell. Blown into at one end with sufficient lung power, it would make a trumpeting blast to sound the alert.

The lady started down the stairs. Before stepping off, Slocum looked down to be sure of his footing. The platform was speckled with dull reddish brown spots. At first, he thought it was some form of moss or lichen, then he realized it was dried blood. A lot of it, shed fairly recently.

The group returned to the village. Lady Xoc pointed out a man she identified as Yax Balam, the tribal chief. The headman's face was lined with pain and he walked hunched forward, taking slow, careful steps.

Slocum went into the hut. He ate a light snack of crabmeat, fruit, and coconut milk mized with mango juice. The meal was served to him by Chicha and Naabi as he lay back in the hammock, nibbling morsels from their dainty hands.

Later, he took a siesta, sleeping through the hottest hours of the day.

When the sun was low, Lady Xoc came to visit. She and Slocum strolled along the beach as shadows grew. They were followed by the omnipresent armed escorts, though Tzotzil was not among them.

As the light failed, fishing boats made for the cove, threading the channels between the reefs. The single-masted sailboats were called *canoas,* Lady Xoc said, not to be confused with canoes, which the tribe also possessed.

Entering the calmer waters of the cove, the canoas drifted into a shallow inlet curving west along the south side of the beach. The freshwater stream emptied into the brackish saltwater. Crewmen jumped overboard, splashing hip deep as they guided the boats to the landing.

The canoas were dragged out of the water and beached on the sand. A knot of tribespeople waited nearby while the crews hauled out their nets, displaying their catch. The slim pickings revealed did not elicit any cheers.

Slocum said, "I guess the fish weren't running today."

"For many days," Lady Xoc said, "but perhaps soon the tide will turn in our favor."

Slocum ate well that night. While the tribe made do with short rations of fish, he enjoyed a special treat. Even before Chicha and Naabi entered the hut with the serving platters, they were preceded by the mouthwatering aroma of freshly roasted meat.

Served on a bed of fruits and vegetables, wrapped in banana leaves, was a succulent roast, spiced and savory. The possum-size carcass was cleaned and dressed, seared, not readily identifiable. Some varmint or other.

Slocum tore off a joint and went to work on it. The meat

was juicy, with a slightly gamy taste he couldn't place. He gnawed sweet flesh off the bone, grease shining on his chin.

As he reached for another piece, sudden intuition made him pause. His hand hovered inches from the platter.

Noting his hesitation, Chicha and Naabi eyed him with mild interest.

Slocum was an outdoorsman and hunter, adept at imitating animal cries. Shrieking like a howler monkey, he pointed at the roast.

Giggling, the girls indicated agreement. His antics provoked their mirth. Nothing in their manner showed that the bill of fare was anything less than a splendid delicacy for an honored guest. Meat was hardly so plentiful on the island that any form of it could be despised.

Besides, the monkey made pretty good eating. No doubt it was the same howler bagged during the morning walk.

Slocum wasn't squeamish. He took another joint from the pile.

"Meat's meat," he said.

The next night was a love feast. It began as a feast of food, but went on to delight all the senses. At the hour of the evening meal, Chicha and Naabi entered the hut, wearing their finest huipils. The dresses were shining white. Embroidery highlighted the garments with bursts of color, like wildflowers in snow. The girls were always clean and well-scrubbed; tonight they must have come fresh from a bath. Hair and skin bore the faint perfumed residue of fragrant cleansing oils.

Slocum himself was minded to dress for the occasion. His sole item of clothing was the cut-off shorts he'd made from his pants. At least they'd had a washing since he'd been cast ashore. He found a narrow woven blue and white blanket, which he draped over his shoulders serape-style.

He thought it added a certain lordly flair to his appearance. Maybe.

He was an important man. That's what Lady Xoc told him. Tonight, he was really getting the royal treatment. Scented candles shed an amber glow. A breeze blew, flowing through the hut by means of the gap between the bottoms of the raised walls and the ground. The candles were in holders attached to hooks on upright wooden pillars. They were raised above the level of the breeze, but occasionally a stray gust would set the candle flames fluttering.

A variety of dishes was laid before him. There was seafood: crabmeat, lobster, clams, sardinelike fish dried in sea salt, fresh fish steamed in banana leaves. Fruit: mangoes, melons, limes, bananas, berries, guava jelly, nuts. Roast duck. Tortillas, aromatic of fresh-ground cornmeal, baked so recently that they were still warm.

And there was pulque, a fiery liquor distilled from the maguey cactus. Unknowing, Slocum tossed back a cup like it was water. The top of his head came off, leaving him red-faced, breathless, and gasping.

Brushing the tears from his eyes, he refilled the little ceramic cup he'd been drinking from.

" 'S good," he said, wheezing. He took only a small sip.

The iguana ran away from the door. A beat or two later, Lady Xoc entered.

Slocum saluted with his pulque cup. Lady Xoc said, "All is to your liking?"

"As fine a feed as I've had anywhere. I couldn't finish this much food in a week, but I'm sure going to try," he said.

"Good, good."

"Not that I'm not grateful, but what's the occasion? Some kind of a feast day or something?"

"You are our honored guest. By honoring you, we honor the sea that brought you here."

"I'd like to get out and meet the people, thank them for helping out a stranger."

"Perhaps soon you will be able to demonstrate your gratitude," she said.

Sometime during the exchange, Slocum's pulque cup had been drained. As soon as he set it down, Naabi refilled it.

"Thanks," Slocum said.

Lady Xoc said, "You like Naabi? She pleases you? And Chicha? She is lovely, no?"

"Why, yes," Slocum said, unsure of how to take her remarks. "They're fine gals."

"They will do anything you want," Lady Xoc said.

"Oh, really?" Slocum was poker-faced.

"Anything you want," she repeated.

"That covers a lot of territory," he said, thoughtful.

"They will pleasure you to your heart's desire, O man from the sea."

The serving girls knelt beside the hammock on which he lay. They sat on their heels, hands folded in their laps, eyes demurely downcast. They may not have known the words, but they knew they were being talked about.

Slocum said, "They know about this, Lady Xoc?"

"To please you is their greatest joy. But if they are not to your taste, other maidens impatiently await your summons," she said.

"Or, if the man from the sea prefers, perhaps a clean young boy . . . ?" she added.

"No," Slocum said. "The girls will be fine."

"Good. You have chosen well. As my handmaidens, they are the fairest in the village. And they have been schooled in all the arts of pleasure."

"Who schooled them? You?"

"A lady excels in all things, O man."

"Come join the party," Slocum said.

Her smile was thin, polite. "Alas, my current ceremonial duties compel me to take a vow of chastity."

"Vows are made to be broken."

She laughed. "How like a gringo! Two women you have yet to enjoy, but you want a third!"

"Well, you've done so much for me, I thought I'd return the favor."

"You are too kind," she said.

She spoke a few final sentences to the girls, who nodded in solemn agreement. She was interrupted by a scuttling sound, as the tethered iguana clawed the dirt in a vain attempt at escape. She gave it a look so cold-blooded that it made the reptile's beady-eyed gaze seem warm by comparison.

The iguana froze. Lady Xoc said, "I leave you to your amours, Sloh Koom."

As she exited, her passage set the candles to flickering. Shadows thrashed, like the beating of giant black wings.

Pausing just inside the door, she said, "The guards have been instructed not to disturb you."

"Good," Slocum said. "Let 'em get their own gals."

Lady Xoc went out. The mood lightened. The iguana began to move about again.

There was a coldness to the lady that made Slocum glad she had declined his invitation. The pulque's heat in his belly and veins melted away any lingering chill.

Studying the bottom of the empty cup, he mused, "I must be getting used to the stuff. When I first started drinking it, it had a kick that makes mezcal look tame. Now, I don't hardly feel it. . . . "

Chicha and Naabi giggled, nudging each other. Slocum realized that he'd been talking to himself.

"Maybe I feel it a little at that," he said.

Refilling the cup to the brim, he offered it to Naabi, who knelt closest to him. She held it in both hands.

He said, "Drink up; it's a party."

Miming the act of drinking, then pointing at the girl, he got the idea across. Naabi sipped, wetting her lips. Her nose wrinkled. Color showed in her face.

Chicha wasn't shy. She took the cup from Naabi and drained it, raising Slocum's eyebrows. She set down the cup. Strands of hair fell across her face. She tossed her head, sweeping the hair back over her shoulders. Her eyes glittered.

Naabi refilled the cup, passed it to Slocum. He caressed her cheek. It was smooth, warm. She took a playful nip at his hand, lightly sinking strong white teeth into his finger.

Now that she had his attention, she took his finger in her mouth and sucked on it.

That really got his attention. Not be outdone, Chicha got into the act. Kneeling beside Naabi, she put an arm around the other's shoulders. Arching her back, she rubbed her pert, pointed breasts against Slocum's arm.

Naabi released Slocum's finger. She licked her lips, slowly and lewdly. Wide lips, broad flat pink tongue.

Chicha took his hand and pressed it to her chest. Her breasts were high and firm. The nipples hardened. He fondled her through her dress, feeling her body heat through the thin fabric.

He still had one hand free, so he fastened it to Naabi's bosom. Her breasts were heavier, fuller than her more girlishly built companion. He squeezed, kneaded them.

It was time to put the hammock to the test. How many could it hold?

Slocum lay on his back in the hammock, a girl on either

side. One arm was around Chicha, the other around Naabi. They lay on their sides, pressing into him. The hammock creaked and swayed, but held up under the strain. Slocum hoped he'd do as well.

A gourdful of pulque rested on his bare chest. The cup lay on its side on the ground, discarded along with the serape. The threesome had long since progressed to drinking the potent brew straight from the gourd's hollow tube-like neck. The girls had some catching up to do to match Slocum, but they were doing their best. It didn't take much pulque to make their cheeks burn and their shining eyes swim in and out of focus.

Chicha and Naabi sprawled against Slocum in drunken abandonment. He was feeling no pain himself. On his right lay Chicha; on his left, Naabi. Chicha's head rested on his shoulder, her long, dark hair spilling across his chest. She lay on her side, with her leg draped across him. Her dress had ridden up to her waist, baring all below. She wore no undergarments. Her shapely thigh pressed against his crotch, rubbing it.

Naabi guzzled from the gourd. Some of it spilled, wetting the front of her dress. Slocum took it from her before more was lost. She giggled. The wet dress clung to her breasts, whose nipples stuck out. Slocum rubbed them.

The gourd felt light. Not much left. Slocum drained it, cast it aside. It landed amid the clay bowls and serving pots that held the remains of the banquet. There was plenty of food left. The heavy gourd broke a ceramic pot lid, shattering it, sending shards flying.

Naabi pulled down the front of her dress, freeing her breasts. She cupped them, rubbing them together, squeezing them so the nipples jutted side by side. The nipples were dark purple-brown with wide areolae.

She rolled over on Slocum, burying his face in her

breasts. He nuzzled them, licking and sucking.

He was hard against Chicha's thigh. She swung her leg off and snuggled in for a closer inspection. The front of his shorts bulged, straining the buttons. She rubbed him with her palm, stroking up and down.

The buttoned fly gave her pause. Slocum figured the island femmes might not be overly familiar with such fasteners, so he helped out by unbuttoning himself. Chicha murmured as his swollen flesh bobbed into view. She gripped him with both hands. Her palms were moist, her fingers skilled.

Naabi smothered him with her breasts. They were damp from the pulque. He tried to mouth her nipples as she rubbed them against his hot, flushed face. They kept slipping free from his sucking mouth.

The hammock heeled, then righted as Chicha put her feet on the ground. She stood, straddling Slocum's hips and the hammock, facing his head. He disengaged from Naabi long enough to wiggle out of his shorts. He rubbed her softly rounded tummy, reached between her plump thighs. Her bush was a triangle of black curls. Her sex was a coral-colored fig, thick-lipped and juicy. Her thighs opened to his touch. He rubbed her between the legs, oozing with liquid heat.

Chicha pulled off her dress, shucking it up and off. She was slender, long-limbed. Her breasts were pear-shaped, with neat round button nipples, sharply pointed. She was slim-hipped, with a fleecy brown pubic triangle, moisture glimmering between delicately shaped lips.

Slocum fisted his rod so that it jutted straight up, its swollen head throbbing. Chicha squatted, legs bending at the knees, bringing her sex down to his.

Slowly, teasingly, she grazed her flesh against his. First

contact was electric, sending Slocum's blood racing. He pressed his cock head between her sex lips, opening her. She was hot and tight. He put a hand on her hip, drawing her to him.

She eased down on him, taking and being taken. The rod swelled, stretched her. Her buttocks tightened convulsively. She mounted the rod, gurgling as it filled her.

Slocum held her hips with both hands. He moved under her. She rocked back and forth. Good as it was, the hammock made it even better, adding its own gravity-defying magic.

Chicha bounced up and down on him. Naabi silenced Slocum's moaning mouth with her breasts. The action peaked.

When he came, lightning snapped his spine like a bullwhip.

Chicha sat up straight, arching her back, throwing her head back, shuddering in spasms. When the spasm passed, she melted, collapsing across him.

Sweat rolled off the lovers, dripping on the dirt floor. Chicha's muscles glistened beneath a sheen of wetness.

Slocum rested, half hard inside her. Naabi rolled off the hammock. She tried to stand, but she was a little too drunk for that. She sank to her knees, eyes rolling. She took off her dress.

The sight of her succulent flesh set Slocum's eyes to rolling.

Naabi's hands were on Chicha, urging her into motion. With drowsily murmured protests, Chicha uncoupled from Slocum. When he popped out of her, she went, "Oh!"

She lay on her side, head resting on an arm, thighs pressed together against oozing inner wetness. Her hair hung down over the side of the hammock, almost touching the floor.

On hands and knees, Naabi crawled to Slocum's middle, her breasts and buttocks jiggling. Her ass was provocative in the extreme, heart-shaped and dimpled. Beneath the cheeks was her wet sex.

Standing on her knees, she leaned over across Slocum. His cock was rubbery in her hands. She palmed, kneaded it. Her face hovered over it. fanning it, with her warm breath. Her hair spilled across his belly and thighs.

She licked her lips. Strength, vigor surged into his flesh, stiffening it even before she took it in her mouth.

She sucked and slurped with single-minded concentration. Her head bobbed, her breasts jiggled. When her head rose, Slocum pulled out of her mouth.

He had other ideas. He got out of the hammock beside her, hooked his hands under her arms, and helped her partially to her feet. She needed help, because she was too drunk to stand up straight. That was okay. She didn't have to stand up for what he had in mind.

Chicha lay curled on her side in the hammock. Slocum moved her legs out of the way, making room for Naabi. He tumbled Naabi into the hammock, so she was kneeling at right angles to it. Her legs were folded under her. Her buttocks rested on the backs of her heels. She folded her arms, snugging them into the side of the sling. She buried her face in them. Her hair hung down over her face, covering it.

Standing on the floor behind her, facing her backside, Slocum reached under her, spreading her knees wider apart. She murmured knowingly as she opened to him. Her head was down and her bottom raised. She wagged it.

Slocum leaned into her. His burning rod throbbed against her juicy buttocks. Taking hold of it, he guided the head to the wet waiting sex beneath the bottom cheeks. He pried her open, entering her. She gasped as he plunged deep.

Her weight was supported by the sling. Taking hold of her hips, he started rocking her back and forth, aided by the pendulumlike sway of the hammock.

Her buttocks jiggled. The hammock's anchoring ropes groaned. He came, groaning.

Other variations followed.

10

It would have been a rough morning after even if they hadn't come for Slocum. But they did.

They came in the weak light of predawn, invading the hut. Lady Xoc, high priest Tata, Tzotzil, and half a dozen warriors. They grouped around Slocum, who lay half-awake, half-asleep in the hammock. The girls slept, too. Their naked limbs were entwined with his.

The trio were shaken awake. Chicha and Naabi disengaged from Slocum. They climbed off the hammock and scampered out of the hut, not bothering to collect their clothes. They left without a word or backward glance, though not without a groan, for they suffered the after-effects of the pulque binge.

Slocum pretended to be more stupefied than he was, though he felt none too sharp. Hard hands pulled him to his feet. His hands were tied in front of him. That was a mistake, one he meant to gain by.

The warriors were small, compactly built. They were armed with machetes, knives, clubs. Tzotzil had a firearm, an old-fashioned blunderbuss. It was three feet long, with a trumpet-shaped mouth. Antique or not, it seemed in good working order. The stock and some of the fittings were new. A blast from it would cut a man in half. He wished Tzotzil didn't seem so eager to use it.

Slocum said, "I'm not your honored guest no more."

"Your visit is at an end, O man," Lady Xoc said.

Tata was impatient for them to be off. Guards formed up around Slocum. Tata started toward the exit. Tzotzil put a hand on Slocum's back and gave him a hard shove.

Slocum stumbled forward, tangled his feet up in the cord tethering the iguana, tripped, and fell. He sprawled head-first, cushioning the impact on his bound forearms.

The cord snapped, freeing the iguana. It took off, trailing about five or six feet of leash.

Lady Xoc spoke sharply, a curt command that the reptile be stopped. A warrior with fast reflexes threw his knife at it, missed. The knife quivered, half buried in the dirt.

The reptile ran out through the gap below the bottom of a raised wall. Tearing across open ground, it disappeared in the brush.

Tata and Lady Xoc exchanged unhappy glances. The reptile's escape was an ill omen. Shaman and witch both believed in the law of sympathetic magic: like begets like. To be brave, eat the heart of a jaguar or a courageous foeman. To be fertile, wear a garment of rabbit fur. The captive reptile had been destined for the cooking pot. Its escape did not augur well for the coming ceremony.

Slocum was hauled to his feet. The guards handled him roughly. Lady Xoc said, "The lizard may have escaped, but you won't."

Tzotzil slammed the butt of his weapon into Slocum's gut. Slocum folded. The guards held him, kept him from falling.

Tata scolded the warrior. It was not for the folk to do violence to the man. From the sea he had come, and to it he belonged. Tzotzil, unimpressed, hastened the proceedings by having his men hustle Slocum outside.

The sky was light, but the sun had not yet risen. The villagers were gathered in the plaza, milling with suppressed excitement. Bright-eyed and happy-faced, they were dressed in their finest festival garb.

An eerie moan sounded, hooting into the morning stillness. It broke the hush again and again, trumpeting low bass notes that vibrated in the pit of one's stomach.

The clarion was a conch shell, sounded by a player who stood on top of the watchtower.

When the last echo died away, Slocum was seized by many hands. They tied him to the litter of driftwood on which he had first been brought to the village.

A procession was formed. At its head was the triumvirate of Yax Balam, Tata, and Lady Xoc. Chief, priest, and witch. Next came Tzotzil and an honor guard of warriors. After them, Slocum and his litter bearers, more warriors, and a trailing of minor personages.

They descended the mound, followed by a mass of villagers. They took the path across the bridge to the landing. From time to time, the trumpeter sounded blasts on his shell.

Slocum lay on his back. His bound hands were clasped at his middle. A rope circled his chest, pinning his upper arms to his sides and his body to the planks. A second rope circled his thighs at the knees.

In the west, the moon was still visible. In the east, pink sky, brightening by the minute.

Slocum's litter tilted from the horizontal to the vertical as he was loaded aboard a canoe. It was thirty feet long, upcurving at bow and stern, with a stepped mast. Part of it was decked over, with a large open space at the stern. Slocum's litter was laid flat on the decking between mast and stern.

On board were Yax Balam, Tata, Lady Xoc, Tzotzil, and a number of warriors doubling as boat handlers. Tow men stood in the shallows of the inlet, holding lines attached to the boat.

The boat slipped its moorings. The tow men hauled on the lines, walking forward into the inlet. Water rose to their knees, their hips, as the boat glided forward.

The water grew too deep to stand and the towlines were taken aboard. Rowers bent to their oars. They struck for the channel. The tide was high and they passed the chain of barrier reefs without incident.

The boat was in open water. The sails were unfurled, trimmed. Breezes swelled the canvas. Oars were shipped. The boat sailed south-southeast. Two boats followed.

Fickle winds caused the boats to take a zig-zag course. The sun rose, a pale yellow disk. For a time, sun and moon were both in the sky. The moon faded, vanished. The sun's disk became a globe, lemon colored, quivering the air in promise of the heat to come.

The crew bent to their tasks. The canoa made all the myriad noises associated with a vessel under sail. Amid the creaks, gurgles, and groans came a soft sawing sound, unnoticed by the crew.

Clasped between Slocum's hands, hidden from view, was a piece of broken pottery. It came from the bowl that had been broken during last night's debauch. He'd palmed it earlier this morning in the hut, when he'd faked the fall for just that purpose. The iguana's getting away was a lucky accident, a welcome distraction, when he'd made his move. No one caught him palming the shard. He held on to it despite being manhandled.

It had sharp edges. He worked it down between his

wrists, where it was hidden by the ropes binding them. The ropes were made of dried plant fibers twined into strands. He sawed away at them from the inside, cutting them so they'd part at the first sharp pull.

The sun rose, grew hot. When spray splashed him, it was a relief. The island dropped from sight.

Seabirds fluttered overhead, circling, screeching. The water changed color, from turquoise to jade. There was a shelf here, with coral masses showing a few fathoms down. On the sea bottom, between the reefs, were forests of kelp. Beds of vertical streamers swayed in the current.

The boats' tackings became labored, growing more exact as the goal neared. The crew was tight-eyed, watchful. They spent a lot of time peering over the side, into the water. Whatever they were looking for, they weren't eager to find it.

Lady Xoc leaned over Slocum. He feared that she'd spotted his subterfuge with the shard.

She said, "Listen to me, Sloh Koom. It is important that you know what is happening to you."

So, she hadn't spotted it. She went on.

"These are the fishing grounds of my people. They are the fields we plow, the sea fields. They supply a rich harvest. But a curse has closed them to us."

"A curse?" Slocum said.

"A curse. A monster," she said. "The Sea Beast."

She said, "The monster was sent by Tlaloc, the water god. You, too, were sent by Tlaloc, O man from the sea. We honor you to honor him. We sheltered you, favored you with our fair daughters."

"Thanks for the hospitality," Slocum said. "You call this sociable?"

"You will not be in discomfort long."

"Why does that fail to comfort me?"

"The time for foolishness is past. Listen carefully, Sloh Koom. When you return to Tlaloc, you will tell him how you fared, how we reverence him through you. Then he will be moved to release us from the curse of his sacred monster."

Slocum said, "You believe that?"

"What matters is that *they* believe." Lady Xoc indicated the other Mayans, in the canoe and the other two boats.

She said, "If true, the curse will be lifted and all will be well. If not—"

She shrugged. "If not, the world will be poorer by one less gringo."

"Yeah? How're you going to do it?"

"You are the sea's, it is forbidden for us to harm you."

"Tell that to the son of a bitch who whomped me in the belly."

"Ah, well, Tzotzil is hot-blooded and allowances must be made," she said. "But you will not be struck again. When we reach the sacred place, you will be returned to the sea from whence you came."

"Drowning, eh?"

"If you're lucky."

"If I'm lucky! And if I'm not?"

"The monster will get you."

"I don't believe in monsters."

"You will, Sloh Koom."

She opened a box whose outside was covered in shark-skin. Inside were small clay jars filled with different colored dyes. She dipped a forefinger into a jar of intense blue-green dye and drew a mark on Slocum's forehead.

He said, "What the hell's this?"

"Ritual," she said, drawing another line. "These are signs sacred to Tlaloc. They mark you as his."

She drew more mystic signs on his face and chest. In

addition to blue-green, the markings were red, yellow, white.

Yax Balam, the chief, sat hunched forward in the stern. His knees were spread wide apart. As the ship rocked on the waves, he winced in pain.

He spoke to Lady Xoc, who speeded up her body painting. Slocum guessed they were nearing their destination. The jagged shard pressed against his sweaty palms.

The oars were manned, backwatering. The boat glided to a halt. A sea anchor was lowered.

The other two boats flanked the first, anchoring a spear's cast apart on either side. The crews spent a lot of time staring worriedly into the water.

Seabirds circled above, some lighting on the mast tops, spars, and rigging. Warriors raised Slocum's litter off the deck, lifting it upright. He sagged against the ropes binding him to the planks. There was some play there. He tensed his muscles, strained against the bonds, relaxed. A subtle process, to avoid detection. He repeated the cycle, falling into a rhythm. Tense/untense. Pause. Tense/untense. Pause.

It was working. There was a lot of give in the plant-fiber ropes. He was stretching them. Gravity helped, too. The ropes around his chest started to ride up. That was too much slack. He puffed out his chest to hold them in place.

This was ritual, with formal aspects. Chief, priest, and witch stood near Slocum on the decking. This patch of sea looked little different from the rest of the shallow banks, of which it was a part. A hundred feet away, three coral humps protruded a few feet above the surface.

Tata prayed and chanted, his voice strong, carrying to the other boats. Slocum hoped he'd take his time. Everyone else on board felt the opposite. They didn't voice their unease, they showed it. They fidgeted, anxiously watching the sea, impatiently glaring at Tata for not finishing.

A ripple disturbed the surface. The Mayans stood on point, quivering, holding their breath. When the disturbance failed to be followed by another, they visibly relaxed.

Tata droned on. More ripples appeared, followed by an upswell of bubbling green froth. Froth churned on the surface. Slocum found himself studying the water as intently as anyone; more so, since he was slated to be going in.

He didn't see much. The water was cloudy, roiled, as if something was stirring up the sea muck.

Something big.

A crewman broke, blurting into Tata's prayers, clearly urging him to hurry up. Tata ignored him, not missing a beat. Yax Balam cast a stern look at the offender, who lowered his head, shamefaced. That wasn't enough for Tzotzil, who cuffed the crewman with the back of his hand, drawing blood from his nose and smashed lips.

Lady Xoc raised her eyes when Tata started into another round. Seabirds leaped screeching from the mast tops, throwing themselves into the sky. Birds already in the air flapped upward, shrieking, climbing.

Tata was stung into speeding up his delivery. The rhythms of his speech indicated he was nearing a big finish. Warriors clutched the edges of the upright litter with white knuckles, awaiting the final syllables of the priest as their cue to jettison the man from the sea back into the sea.

Above wheeled the shrieking birds. A swell lifted the boat. Mayans fought for balance, grabbing handholds.

Bubbles streamed to the surface, fizzing, foaming, bringing up strands of seaweed. Now Slocum could see something. It looked as if a section of sea bottom had detached itself to float to the surface.

Disk shaped, it was as wide across as the boat was long. It had horns, wings, and a tail.

Devilfish.

Slocum had seen one like it, once, while sailing up the Sea of Cortes between Mexico and Baja California, en route to the mouth of the Colorado River on an ill-fated gold hunting expedition. The thing was a giant manta ray, called a devilfish because of the two hornlike protuberances on top of what passed for its head. Slocum had been damned glad when the thing veered away, rather than investigate the ship. And that specimen had been less than half the size of the monster now flapping toward the surface.

On the other boats they were pointing and shouting. Tata shouted too, spraying flecks of spittle as he roared into the climax. The warriors who held Slocum on the litter shook with eagerness to throw him over the side.

The priest finished. Slocum squeezed in his exit line: "Wait till I tell Tlaloc about you!"

Lady Xoc was the only one who got it, and she was more concerned with getting to the side of the boat opposite the one facing the devilfish.

The warriors prepared to give Slocum the heave. He tugged against his wrist bonds. They didn't break. The litter was being lifted off the deck.

Furious, he tried again. This time, the precut ropes snapped.

One of the men shouted. Slocum backfisted him in the belly, He folded up, letting go of his part of the litter. That end of it hit the deck.

The devilfish surfaced, whitewater circles fanning out from it, foamy brine sluicing off its black-speckled, gray-brown back, which shimmered like wet silk. It was pancake shaped, with a blunt-edged front and tapering tail. Near the tip of its leading edge rose two short curved horns. Its eyes were fist-size black orbs. Its wings fluttered with slow, rippling sweeps.

It surged toward the boat. Its wide, lipless mouth gaped, seaweed dangling from the corners. Sticking out of its back was the rusted black iron barb of a harpoon, long buried in its flesh.

Despite their name, devilfish generally shy away from humans. This monster was big enough to take the fight to them. No doubt the painful barb was a permanent goad to the creature.

The pot shard was clenched in Slocum's fist. The other hand was empty. Tata stumbled into him. He grabbed Tata's wrist as the litter started to go over.

As the water rushed up to meet him, he pulled Tata along, over the side.

He gulped a breath before the splashdown. Tata's outcry was silenced as he plunged beneath the waves.

The litter sank. Slocum let go of Tata. Tata kicked for the surface. Slocum kept going down.

Slocum sank. Tata splashed. Despite his age, he was a strong swimmer, but fear made him clumsy. The sea beast veered toward him. He churned up the water as he made for the boat. Crewmen shouted, ready to push him off if he reached the side.

The giant manta's edges fluttered like the folds in a cloak. Its wings made powerful sweeps. A downstroke sucked Tata beneath the surface. Water filled his screaming mouth.

A platform interrupted his descent and he was borne upward, out of the water. He crouched on the back of one of the manta's wings. It was smooth, porous, alive.

Water ran out of Tata's mouth, enabling him to scream again.

Abruptly, the giant shrugged, giving its wing a little flip. Tata was flicked off, catapulted into the air. He flew over the boat, splashing down beyond its far side.

A few fathoms below the surface, Slocum struggled to get free. Pressure squeezed his eardrums and lungs. The water was murky with silt stirred up by the creature.

Slocum had stopped sinking. The natural buoyancy of the litter had stabilized his descent. Soon he would begin to rise.

That was worse. Up was where the devilfish was.

He got his hands under the bottom strand of the chest ropes and pushed up. Ropes scraped his skin. He wriggled out from under them.

Now his upper body was free. His lungs felt ready to burst. There was a thump from below. The planks had struck a coral outcropping. He was near the bottom.

He grabbed the ropes binding his legs and pushed down. Once they were past his knees, it was easy to kick free. The planks rose without him.

He struck for the surface. Darkness interlaced his vision. Lack of oxygen was getting to him.

Above were two great shadows, those of the devilfish and the boat. Slocum avoided both. The shadows came together with a bump as the devilfish rammed the boat. Hollow echoes boomed through the water.

Slocum's head broke the surface. Everything was night-black. The darkness was shot through with suns, giant ones, red and yellow and blue.

He sucked air. The suns dimmed, shrank. Darkness melted, replaced by the reality of blue sky, green sea. He got more air, and the stars dwindled to colored dots dancing before his eyes.

He'd surfaced astern of the boat. He swam away from it. Those on the boat were too busy to notice him. They had their hands full with the monster.

Somebody on one of the other boats saw him, shouted. But neither of those boats was coming any closer.

Slocum put the boat between him and the monster. A body floated nearby: Tata.

At first, Slocum thought he was dead. But Tata was only stunned. He managed to stay afloat and keep his head above water. Slocum would have finished him off, but he wasn't worth the effort it would take to drown him.

The giant ray got under the boat and surfaced. The boat heeled over on her starboard beam. It hung, on the verge of capsizing, but the ray couldn't do it.

The manta submerged. The boat righted, raising a splash—a big one. A few crewmen were flung into the water. The rest held on for dear life.

The manta's tail whipped out of the water. It was long, muscular, with a barbed tip. It lashed across the deck, sending men flying.

Swimming alongside the boat, the manta slung a wingtip over the gunwale. Wood strained, splintered. The monster put some weight into it, pulling down. The boat tilted, heeling to port, flipping more of the crew into the water.

Tzotzil prodded the wingtip with a short spear. With a violent shudder, the wingtip retracted. The boat righted. Only a few people were left on board. The rest flailed about in the water, trying to escape the monster.

The devilfish quivered, favoring its wounded flap. Its eyes were emotionless, but its gill slits worked agitatedly.

Tzotzil cast his spear at it. The blade struck a bony plate between its horns. It bounced off, but not before gouging a deep furrow in the beast's hide.

The manta reared up showing its white underside as it shied away from the boat. Its thrashings created high waves, swamping those who had gone overboard. When the waves passed, all of the swimmers were still there.

One knot of swimmers was clustered to the creature's right side. The manta went for them, charging. At the last second before impact, it peeled off to the left, raising its right wing out of water.

The wing hung over the swimmers' heads, blotting out the sun. The heads screamed as the wing came down, blotting them out.

There was a tremendous smacking sound as the wing slapped the water. Those caught beneath it were crushed.

The manta went left, closing on the other group of swimmers. They swam harder than ever, not getting far. The manta glided among them, smashing them with its wings, flipping bodies into the air.

Slocum swam toward the boat's starboard side. Those few still on board looked to port, where the manta was.

Slocum hauled himself up over the side and climbed, dripping, into the boat. A handful of Mayans remained, including Lady Xoc. She lay prone on the deck, clinging to the base of the mast. By some miracle, the mast was still intact.

She saw Slocum, shouted warning to the others. Slocum dropped into the stern. There was a tillerman, a warrior, and Yax Balam. They turned to confront him. The warrior had a knife. The chief had a war club knobbed with a gray-green stone carved in the shape of a frog's head.

Tzotzil, crouching at the bow, started astern.

Slocum grabbed an oar, held it in both hands, a long ungainly thing. He hit the warrior on the head, breaking off the blade. It wasn't so ungainly anymore.

Something flashed in the corner of his eye. Slocum stepped back, dodging the knife thrown at him by Lady Xoc. It wheeled past, burying itself with a thud in the chest of the startled tillerman.

Lady Xoc didn't waste time with apologies. She looked for another knife.

The tillerman stared down at the knife in his chest. He

opened his mouth, coughed, spat blood. He slumped, collapsed.

Slocum thrust the jagged edge of the oar at the chief. Yax Balam parried with the club, knocking it aside. Slocum followed through, slashing with the other end. It slammed the chief in the head, sending him staggering. Slocum used the pole to knock him over the side.

Tzotzil charged, holding a machete. He was nimble, surefooted. Slocum jabbed with the jagged end of the pole, keeping Tzotzil at bay. Tzotzil danced just out of reach, searching for an opening.

Lady Xoc crawled to Slocum and threw her arms around his knees. He cursed. Tzotzil lunged, thrusting the machete like a short sword. Slocum parried, wood ringing on steel.

Lady Xoc grabbed at his groin. He kneed her in the head, stunning her. She clung to his legs.

Tzotzil thrust, slipping inside Slocum's guard. Slocum recoiled, fell, the point of the machete grazing his middle. He had to suck in his gut to avoid it.

He fell into the stern, entangled with Lady Xoc. He still had the pole. He swung it upward, between Tzotzil's legs.

Tzotzil whoomphed, jackknifed. His face was leaden, his eyes sick. Slocum swept the pole to one side, knocking Tzotzil's foot out from under him. Tzotzil fell backward.

Lady Xoc grabbed the pole with both hands, forcing it down.

"Damn you!" Slocum said.

Tzotzil rose shakily. Behind him, the manta surfaced near the boat. It was quiet, raising barely a ripple to disturb the bodies surrounding it. It eyed Tzotzil, perhaps recalling the spear he had thrown. Pain from that age-old harpoon barb buried in its back served as a nagging reminder of what the surface dwellers could do.

Holding the machete in both hands, Tzotzil raised it

above his head. The manta struck, lashing out with its tail. The spiny barbed tail speared Tzotzil in the back.

It pierced him, spiking a gory tip through his chest.

Lady Xoc groaned in horror.

Its tail upcurving like a scorpion's, the manta raised Tzotzil off his feet, into the air. The tail was taut as a bent sapling. Tzotzil, impaled, was held writhing over its head.

After a steady inspection, the monster got rid of Tzotzil, tossing him with a flick of its tail.

Lady Xoc crawled on hands and knees to the stern. Slocum moved to intercept her. He reached her as she pulled the knife from the tillerman's chest.

Before she could stab upward into his belly, Slocum punched her in the jaw. The short, sweet jab landed square on the point of her chin with an audible pop.

Lady Xoc's eyes rolled up and she went limp. Slocum took the knife from her nerveless hand. He wiped it clean on the tillerman's shoulder.

Slocum rolled Lady Xoc on her back and positioned her with her head and shoulders wedged upright. No drowning for her in the water sloshing in the bottom of the boat. He wanted her alive.

Slocum clambered to the bow. He used the knife to saw at the anchor rope. Mayans in the other boats saw what he was doing and set up a howling. They were content to steer clear of the fight with the devilfish, but they didn't want to see Slocum get away.

Spears flew in his direction. A few came damned close, one thudding into the deck eighteen inches from his head. His teeth hummed from the vibration.

The anchor line parted. The boat lurched to starboard, propelled by the manta's turbulent motions.

Slocum jumped up. The nearest boat swung toward his. Crewmen bent to the oars. Others made threatening gestures with knives and clubs. They must have loosed all their spears with the first cast. He was glad that the sea voyage had precluded their bringing any firearms along. From what he had seen of them, they were dead shots. They had to be, with ammunition so precious that they used not lead but stone pellets.

He wrenched the spear loose from the deck. It was four feet long, with one-quarter of it taken up by the stone blade.

Slocum threw it. It flew staight and true, spearing an oarsman through the cheek. The other rowers were thrown off stride.

Slocum went back to the stern. The boat on that side was making for him, too, but it was farther away.

The tillerman was dead weight. Slocum lowered him gently over the side opposite the monster, to avoid attracting its notice.

He grabbed the tiller, pointing the bow away from the wind. Working the tiller back and forth caused the rudder to act something like a paddle, speeding up the turn.

Mayans shouted threats and curses. That decided the devilfish, which had been idling, studying the scene. One boat had been mostly purged of its complement of noisy surface dwellers, with their painful stings. The other boats were full of them.

The devilfish made for the boat off Slocum's bow. It's great sweeps flapped, gathering speed. It cut a V-shaped wake as it surged toward its target.

The crew pointed, hollered. Some lined the rail, wielding oars like lances to repel the monster.

The devilfish charged, rearing just before it was about to strike the boat amidships. Oars splintered like twigs against it. Its leading edge crashed down on the side.

Timbers broke, boards popped. The boat tilted, dragged down by the creature's weight. Her opposite side curved up, heeling, throwing men into the sea. Water rushed in through the damaged hull, further weighing her down.

The decks were awash. The boat sank to the top of her gunwales. The mast broke.

A few of the crew clung to the wallowing hulk, but most were in the water. The devilfish went among them.

Wind filled the sail of Slocum's boat, nudging it away from the scene, westward. Slowly.

The other boat tried to escape, too. It was almost on the manta when the decision was made to change course. The manta changed course, pursuing her. The crew's shouts irked the beast, though nowhere near as much as their spears.

The devilfish dived, nosing down, its delta-shaped body curling after. Choppy water swallowed up its barbed tail and it was gone, vanished.

Not for long. It surfaced with the boat on its back, lifting her clear out of the water, then setting her down urgently. The beast had great sport mangling those who had been cast overboard.

The boat was crippled, dead in the water. Some on board were still alive. With one boat smashed and another on the run, the devilfish could linger over this last conquest.

While the monster turned her to driftwood, Slocum got away.

11

Slocum was at sea, again. At least this time, he was on a boat. A lot of boat. Too much boat, and too little boatman. At first, he just ran south, away from the monster. If the devilfish had wanted to overtake him, it could have. It didn't. Long after it had dropped below the horizon, Slocum dreaded its reappearance. It could surface anywhere, anytime, without warning.

With the wind at his back, it was a brisk run. The boat was going too fast, racing into unknown waters. It took muscle to hold the tiller steady; it kept wanting to go its own way. Slocum had trouble keeping an even keel. The boat's speed was nerve-racking. It was good for escaping the monster, but now he'd have liked to be able to slow down.

The boat came close to capsizing. Slocum wrestled her back on course, but it had been close.

He turned out of the wind, gradually. Air slipped from the slackening sail. The boat slowed.

Slocum let out his breath. He said, "I hate boats."

The boat rode on the waves, in no immediate danger. Slocum moved to get everything shipshape and squared away.

Lady Xoc was still knocked out. At least she seemed to be; she could be playing possum. Her hands were empty. There were no weapons within reach. He patted her down for concealed weapons and found none. He felt around at the top of her head, wrecking her elaborate hairdo. It hadn't come away from the devilfish encounter in too good shape, anyhow. Those long black tresses could have been hiding a lethal needle or straight pin, but they weren't.

She groaned. Before she came to, Slocum tied her up. He examined the boat's stores. There were two large sealed jugs of fresh water, and supplies of dried fish and dried fruit, enough to last for a long time.

Slocum collected all the weapons. He took a short spear, machete, and two obsidian knives. The rest he stowed away.

He loosened the rigging of the sail with a blade, to keep the boat from foundering in too-strong winds. They were none too strong now, and it had been all he could do to handle the sails.

Time for a talk with Lady Xoc.

He filled a bucket with seawater and poured it on her face. She came to, sputtering and choking, when the pail was half empty, but Slocum gave her the rest.

She was mad, but there wasn't much she could do about it, not with her hands and feet tied. Slocum let her rage for a while, till he got bored. He picked her up and hung her over the side, her head down and in the water.

When he let her up for air, she was quiet. Not tamed, just quiet.

Slocum said, ''The gods punished you.''

Whatever she was expecting to hear, that wasn't it. Her reaction was a gasp of disbelieving laughter.

''You're mad!'' she said.

''Those who tried to kill me are dead, killed by the monster they meant to sacrifice me to," Slocum said. "Am I not the man from the sea?"

"Absurd!"

"I lived and the others died. If that's not the will of the gods, what is it?"

"This would be blasphemous if it were not so ridiculous," she sniffed. "Gringo of the gods? Hah!"

"Maybe it's a test of faith . . . and you're failing."

She looked past him, at the sea. No land in sight. Slyness crept into her expression.

She said, "Your kingdom awaits, O man from the sea."

"I could toss you overboard right now."

"But you do not. Why not? Because you need me alive. Why?"

"You tell me."

"Because you're lost," she said.

"Not that lost," he said. "I know I'm somewhere off the coast of Yucatán. If I go south long enough, sooner or later I'll reach Belize or British Honduras."

She sneered. "You will die long before then. You need me, Sloh Koom. I know where we are."

"How much water can you breathe before telling me everything I want to know?"

She shrugged.

"Not much, I can tell you," he said.

"Whatever the gods will."

"Don't give me that. You're too fond of yourself to throw your life away."

She leaned against the side of the boat. Her hands were tied behind her back. Her feet were tied, too. She had to make numerous minute adjustments of position to maintain her balance.

She said, "What do you propose?"

"What's the nearest town?"

"That's a question, not a proposal."

"Get me to the nearest settlement, and I'll let you live. A real town, with a fort and a harbor."

"A vecino town," she said.

"I didn't do so well among the Maya."

"Was it we who sank your ship and made you a castaway? It was your own kind, Sloh Koom."

"You talk like you know something."

"You talked in fever dreams, when you were fresh from the sea. In English. Again and again, you said the word *pirates*. Close enough to the Spanish, *piratos*, for me to catch the meaning."

"So?"

"You are right to fear the pirates. They could come upon us at any time."

"Then why are you smiling?"

"I did not know I was. No matter."

"If the pirates come, you won't live to greet them, lady."

"I would prefer it that way. I do not wish to fall alive into their hands."

"You're talking sense. Tell me where to point this boat and we'll be on our way," Slocum said.

"What will I get in return?" Lady Xoc said.

"Your life."

She shook her head. "When I tell you what you need to know, you will kill me."

"No. I'll need you alive in case you've lied."

"When you're sure I've told the truth, then you will kill me."

"If your words are true, I'll let you go."

"Why should I trust you?"

"Because I'm the man from the sea."

Lady Xoc decided. "Very well. Ciudad Aurora lies a day's sail to the south."

"Good. If true."

"It's true, gringo. I tell you that, not because I trust you, but because of what I have not told you. There is something else you will need to know to reach the city."

"What?"

"I'll tell you when the time comes. That will give you a reason to keep me alive until then."

"Okay," Slocum said, "for now."

He made ready to get under way. She sneered at his inept seamanship.

He said, "You folks had me bothered for a while. There I was, a stranger, alone and friendless, washed up on your island more dead than alive. You took me in, sheltered me, fed me. Not to mention those other creature comforts. I knew there was a catch, but I couldn't figure out what it was. Not until you tossed me to the biggest damned devilfish in all creation. Then I knew you'd saved me so you could feed me to your monster.

"Restored my lack of faith in human nature, it did," he said.

Seated in the bottom of the boat, Lady Xoc squirmed uncomfortably.

"Those ropes must hurt," Slocum said.

"Yes, they do."

"Good."

Slocum sailed south-southwest. The boat wallowed along at a speed of a few knots. She could do much more, but that's all that Slocum felt comfortable with. The big boat rode the waves well enough, but it was hard to handle.

Lady Xoc didn't think much of his boat handling skills and told him so. Often. Some of her suggestions were practical, helping him to better control the boat. It would have been simpler to let her do it, but she was too dangerous to be left unrestrained.

A fuzzy green line showed in the west. Land. The sight of it cheered Slocum. The open sea wasn't for him. He was a coast-hugger. At worst, he could ground the boat, go ashore, and continue on foot.

He sailed south, keeping the coast on his right side. He ran offshore at the near limits of visibility, to avoid being seen by islanders or coast dwellers. No other craft were at sea.

Lady Xoc complained of her bonds. Slocum tied a noose at one end of a length of line. He fitted the noose around her neck. He cut her hands free. She groaned with the pain of stiff joints suddenly released. She caught herself and stifled all further sounds of discomfort, though she must have been hurting. She'd been tied a long time.

She shook out her shoulders, loosening them. She chafed rope-burned wrists, rubbing them to ease the soreness. She waited for him to free her feet, but he didn't do it. She wasn't having her hands and feet free at the same time.

Slocum handed her a gourd dipper, brimming with fresh water from a cask. She drank from it, holding it in both hands. She winced from the pain of where he'd socked her on the chin. She stroked it, feeling the contours of the bruise. She looked down, not quick enough to hide the murder in her eyes.

Slocum chuckled. "You'd like to cut out my heart and eat it."

She didn't deny it. She ate some dried fruit, sipped some more water. When she was done, Slocum put away the gourd. He retied her hands and untied her feet. Later, he retied them. It was tempting to keep the noose around her neck, but he took it off as a gesture of good faith. She wasn't impressed.

Fair winds made for smooth sailing. The day waned. Slocum spied a few specks on the water that might have been boats. He made for the open sea. The specks dwindled, vanished, and did not reappear.

Slocum sailed south for some leagues before once more turning shoreward. The sun was low, shining straight into his eyes, blinding. A fleet could come out of the sun at him and he wouldn't see it until it was too late.

He went back out to sea. The sun set.

Purple twilight.

Slocum said, "How far?"

"We are not even halfway there," Lady Xoc said. "We would have been much closer had you not followed a drunkard's course."

"These days I'm sticking close to land."

Venus shone in the west, not far from the horizon. Other stars came out, shimmering in the deep blue sky. Darkness fell. The stars brightened. The constellations were subtly altered due to the nearness of the equator, but Slocum knew most of them, anyway. Heavenly beacons to steer by.

Moonrise. The silver sea seemed peaceful, but Slocum knew better.

After an hour, Lady Xoc grew restless. She spoke, breaking a long silence.

"Sloh Koom . . ."

"Yes?"

"Has it occurred to you that the gods want me to live?"

"I haven't given it much thought."

"I was saved for a purpose."

He laughed. "I'll say you were! And if we don't reach Aurora, your usefulness is over."

"Kill me and you kill your luck."

"Nobody's killing nobody. Yet." He eyed her more keenly.

He said, "Why talk about killing? Unless you know something I don't."

"Below the horizon is an island," she said. "The island of the pirates."

"Ah. I thought you knew more about them than you were telling."

She shrugged. "My people are fisher folk. We know what happens on the sea around us. The island is an empty rock inhabited by scorpions and seabirds. But there's a good harbor and fresh water springs."

Slocum shook his head. "A spot like that wouldn't be uninhabited. Too useful. Try again."

"It is a sacred spot, a shrine! No Maya would settle there. A year ago, the pirates came. They made it their base. Soon after, the Sea Beast invaded our fishing grounds. The elders believe it was a punishment visited on us by Tlaloc, angry at profanation of his island shrine."

"But we know better, eh?"

"Who can say? The Sea Beast was unknown to us before the coming of the pirates."

"Let it go," Slocum said. "We've got to pass this pirate isle?"

"Yes."

He grimaced at the moonlight. "Too bright now. We'll have to wait till the moon goes down."

He sailed on until an island notched the horizon. "That's it?"

"Yes, Sloh Koom."

"This's close enough. Now we wait."

He hauled a heavy stone out of the ballast at the bottom of the boat to replace the anchor he'd lost while escaping the devilfish. He tied a line to the stone. He also tied on a spar. The bottom here was too deep to sound, but the spar would provide added drag for the sea anchor. He lowered it over the side.

Slocum untied her. They ate. This time she ate the dried fish as well as the fruit. Time passed. The moon was a long time waning. Slocum wanted sleep, but he stayed awake.

The moon was still high in the west when Slocum prepared to go. It was after midnight, he guessed. Too bright for his liking, but he dare not delay any longer. He wanted that pirate isle well over the horizon before first light.

Slocum bound Lady Xoc. She said, ''You don't have to do that.''

He said, ''Well . . .''

He left her tied and hauled anchor. That was a job. It left him panting. He rigged the sail. He took the tiller. The boat moved.

Slocum sailed south-southeast, angling out to sea, to get even farther from the isle when he passed it. He went too far out and had some trouble getting back in. His boat-handling was clumsy, at times dangerous.

Lady Xoc cursed. ''Fool! Untie me and let me take the helm before you sink us!''

''No,'' Slocum said.

He didn't trust her, not with the tiller in her hands. She might sink the boat and take her chances with the sea. Most islanders could swim like fish.

The boat rode out the effects of his last wrong move. She wallowed along more or less on course, sailing south past the seaward side of the isle.

That's where the harbor was, on the seaward side, according to Lady Xoc. There were lights at the water's edge. The boat was well beyond their reach. Bursts of noise carried across the water.

Slocum studied the rocky isle, memorizing its outline as

best he could, fixing it against the constellations for future reference.

No alarm was raised, no pursuit given. The boat sailed on, undetected. The island fell behind, lingering on the horizon for a maddeningly long time before disappearing.

Slocum made for the coast. With it in sight, he could never be too far lost. Hell, if he had to, he'd point himself north on dry land and walk to Texas.

He wouldn't really walk, not all that way. He'd steal a horse first. But not before he settled certain business matters and personal grudges.

12

Slocum reached Dawn City at noon. Ciudad Aurora was a small but busy port on the northeast coast of the Bahia de la Ascencion. The bay was a deepwater anchorage big enough to accommodate a fleet of one of the world's great navies. There was no such fleet in place—yet.

A fort built in the days of the conquistadores stood on a hill overlooking the town. On a lower height, but still above the town, was a mission-style church. The town itself was a jumble of whitewashed cubes, dazzling in the sunlight.

A river poured brown water into the harbor. A few tall ships stood at anchor. None of them was the black-sailed pirate ship, the *Perla Negra*.

A variety of small craft crisscrossed the harbor on various errands. Skiffs, canoes, rowboats, canoes. Slocum avoided them. He pointed the bow toward the mud flats west of town.

The shore neared. Slocum approached Lady Xoc, knife in hand. She lay curled in the stern, all trussed up. The obsidian blade was a black mirror with a razor edge.

She got ready to spit in his eye. He forestalled that by getting behind her. He cut her bonds.

"Looks like I'll have to forgo the pleasure of cutting your throat," he said, "not that you don't deserve it."

She sagged from relief or fatigue, maybe both. No sounds of pain escaped her, not a groan or a whimper, though she had to be hurting. Hours had passed since she had last been untied.

Slocum moved opposite her, where he could cover her if she tried anything. Her limbs were stiff, clumsy. Her face was smooth, blank, with hot, hard eyes. She rubbed her arms and legs to restore circulation.

She said, "Am I supposed to be grateful?"

"Lady, you ain't supposed to be nothing a-tall. I just don't want you bleeding in my boat."

He gestured with the knife, adding, "Which doesn't mean I won't gut you like a fish if you move wrong."

"Filthy gringo!"

"Is that any way to talk about the man from the sea?"

She lapsed into Mayan, speaking heatedly. A frequently used word was *tahol*. Whatever it meant, it wasn't nice.

When she quieted down, Slocum said, "When you get home, you'll have to do some tall talking to explain how I got away from the devilfish."

That started her up again. When she ran out of steam, Slocum said, "Git."

She stared, uncomprehending.

The shore was a few hundred yards distant. Slocum said, "You can swim the rest of the way. Good-bye!"

She jumped to her feet, spat, and dove off the side. She swam underwater, smooth limbs flashing. She was a good distance away before she surfaced. She breathed, ducked down below, and continued swimming to shore. She swam at a tangent to the boat's course.

Land neared. About fifty yards from shore, the boat

grounded on a sandbar, the impact throwing Slocum forward.

''That's one way of making landfall,'' he said.

The boat was stuck fast, beyond his means of getting it free. Beyond the bar, the water was shallow enough for him to wade ashore.

The flat was a long, muddy strip, bounded on the west by the river mouth and on the east by the wharves of the waterfront district. At the far edge of the strip was a scattering of ramshackle huts. A few people, not many, were out on the flat. It was hot.

Lady Xoc came ashore. She disappeared in the bushes at the top of the flat.

The boat was grounded, but not if the tide rose. Slocum dropped anchor, handling the heavy stone with authority. His strength was coming back.

There wasn't much of value on board, but the machetes were good and the obsidian daggers might be worth something to collectors. He made up a packet of dried fish and dried fruit. Weapons and food were wrapped in a carryall made from a blanket knotted at the ends.

The best machete and dagger he kept for himself. To the pommels, he tied thin tough ropes, looping them into slings. He slung the dagger around his neck and the machete over his shoulder. Hefting the blanket, he went over the side.

The water was up to his thighs. He stepped off the sandbar. The water rose to his chest. It lowered as he slogged ashore.

The people on the flat melted away. When he set foot on dry land, there wasn't a soul in sight. Slocum started east, toward town. A yellow dog with its ribs showing trotted out from behind a shanty and yelped at him. He continued walking. The dog rushed at his back. He reached for the machete. The dog retreated, yipping.

It felt funny to be walking after a day and night at sea. Slocum's legs were rubbery. The machete felt good, swinging at his side. A brace of Colts would have felt better.

Ahead, gulls pecked at a dead thing that had washed up on the beach. They pecked at each other, squabbling over who got what. Others hovered overhead, screeching. All ignored Slocum, save for one strutting on the sidelines. As Slocum walked by, it lunged at him. He had to step lively to keep from being pecked.

"I'll cut your damned head off!" he said.

The bird squawked, not retreating. Slocum had a mental picture of himself chasing it with a machete. Instead, he walked faster.

Through a screen of fluttering white wings, he glimpsed the carrion the birds fed on: a bloated, hairless quadruped with hoofed feet and a long ratlike tail, like a cross between a pig and a possum.

Shacks and shanties along the flat gave way to more solid structures as he neared the docks. He walked along the brush, in the shade. The sea shimmered like boiling mercury.

Over the tops of warehouses he saw tall ship masts and crosstrees. He entered the waterfront district. There were piers and wharves, storehouses, stacked cargo bales. A dirt road ran parallel to the water. Its landward side was lined with a row of buildings: flophouses, whorehouses, dives. Nobody was outside. The sun was at its height.

Flies buzzed around mounds of stinking garbage between the buildings and in the street. Stuccoed walls were cracked, yellowed. Doorways opened on brown-shadowed interiors. Somewhere, someone picked at a guitar, not playing it, just picking it.

Slocum slowed in front of a shop. The building looked like a pitted cube of brown sugar. Through dirty glass windows he saw a space cluttered with merchandise. He brushed aside the beaded curtain hanging in the doorway and went in.

The shop was hot and dim, smelling of rope, grease, wood. A combination trading post and general store. A window opened in the rear wall. There was no glass in it. An Indian sat under it, braiding a rope.

His black hair was cut in a bowl shape. He wore a white shirt and white pants. His feet were bare. He stood up and went out the back door.

A man came in. He was heavyset, with a big gut. A holstered gun hung high on his right hip.

Three-inch boot heels clattered as he came up the aisle into the shop. He smelled of sweat, tobacco, and tequila.

He said, "What you want, gringo?"

Slocum laid the blanket on the counter and unwrapped it, displaying the machetes and knives.

"Thought we might do a trade," Slocum said.

The other condescended to glance at the blades. "Nothing there for me," he said. "I might be able to give you a little something for the machetes."

"Sure," Slocum said.

Nando, the shopkeeper, was in the mood to dicker. That suited Slocum. It was better than being out in the sun. Nando showed no surprise at dealing with the half-naked stranger. Such things happened on the waterfront. Why ask questions?

Slocum's Spanish was better than Nando's English, so they spoke Spanish. The machetes were of a finer quality than any of the store's stock. Nando betrayed his interest in them by his elaborate disinterest. He waved away the daggers, saying, "No Indian stuff."

Slocum left them in place. The dickering continued. Sweat poured off Nando, soaking his shirt. "This is thirsty work," he said. Slocum agreed. Nando led him out the back of the shop into a yard.

A wooden plank table stood under a vine-covered trellis. The space was pleasant, well-shaded. The two men sat down.

Nando called for tequila. The servant brought it. A Mayan, he lacked the martial vigor of the warlike People of the Sea. He was tamed—or so he seemed.

Nando filled two glass tumblers with tequila. Slocum's glass was dirty, like its twin. Tequila fumes stung his eyes. Nando raised his glass, saying, "Saludos."

"Your health," Slocum seconded.

They drank. No worry about the dirty glass. The tequila was strong enough to vaporize the toughest germ.

They drank some more. Slocum broke out a packet of dried fish and fruit and shared it. It was something to chew on between rounds. Negotiations went back and forth. Tequila, too.

The bottle was low and the sun was, too, when the two men finally came to terms. More out of mutual exhaustion than anything else. Mutual drunkenness. Each swore that the other had skinned him, so the trade must have been fairly equal.

No sooner was the deal struck than an idea took form in Slocum's head, surviving the attempts of the tequila to dissolve it.

He said, "Want to buy a boat?"

"No, no," Nando said. "What kind of boat?"

"I'll show you," Slocum said.

They went outside, in front of the store. Slocum said, "You can see it from the top of the flat."

When they reached the vantage point, the boat was nowhere to be seen. Waves rolled over the spot where it had run aground.

Where was the boat? Probably sailing north with Lady Xoc at the helm. Once the tide had refloated the boat, all she had to do was cut the anchor line and head out to sea.

Slocum shrugged. He and Nando trudged back to the shop. Something nagged at Slocum's mind. What had Lady Xoc called him? *Tahol?*

Indicating the servant, Slocum said, "Ask him what *tahol* means."

The Mayan giggled. Nando said, "I can tell you that. *Tahol* is, how you say, a *cabeza de mierdra . . . ?*"

"Shithead," Slocum said.

"*Si.*"

"Uh-huh. Well, we'll see."

The room was dark except where moonlight shone in through the windows. Chobham crossed to his desk. He knew the layout of his study well enough to avoid bumping into any unseen obstacles. He struck a match, lighting a lamp. Its globe was a golden ball, underlighting his face. He turned up the wick, and light filled the room.

A man sat in an armchair facing the desk. A stranger. How long had he been sitting there in the dark?

The man held a gun, a hand cannon. Its big black bore was aimed at Chobham.

Chobham's mouth fell open.

The stranger put a finger across his lips, signaling silence. "Shhh," he said.

He was a gringo, like Chobham. He wore a straw planter's hat, shirt, loose-fitting pants, and sandals. He was sunburned, hollow-cheeked, with a ten-day beard.

On a table beside him was a decanter of vintage brandy, which Chobham reserved for special guests, and a brandy glass. There wasn't much brandy left.

The stranger rose, covering Chobham with the gun. He

came around the desk. Holding the gun to Chobham's side, he patted him down, frisking him for weapons. He found a short-barreled revolver and pocketed it.

He backed away, crossing to the door, locking it. He motioned Chobham to move out from behind the desk.

He said, "Sit."

Chobham's knees were watery. He sank down into the armchair so recently vacated by the intruder.

The stranger sat behind Chobham's desk. He laid the hand cannon on its side on the desk, pointing at Chobham.

He said, "Drago sent me."

Chobham frowned. He was a soft-fleshed, pleasant-faced young man, balding, with curly reddish gold side whiskers and mustache.

"Drago? The pirate?" he said.

"You know him, then," the stranger said.

"I know of him. Who in this part of the coast doesn't? But I've had no dealings with the man."

"No?"

"No. Meaning no disrespect to the captain, of course," Chobham said quickly. "You must be mistaking me for someone else."

"You're Arthur Chobham, local agent for Yankee gun-runners."

"You're—" On the verge of making a denial, Chobham thought better of it and switched gears in midsentence.

"—You're very well-informed," he said. He leaned forward, hands on thighs. "Is that what this is all about? Munitions?"

"Pirates can't have too many guns," said the stranger.

Chobham sat back, racked by greed and fear. Greed won. He said, "It may be possible to come to some sort of an arrangement. Our firm is always on the lookout for new clients . . ."

Chobham's tension had begun to ease now that the talk had turned to business matters. It was ratcheted back up to the breaking point by the stranger's next remark.

"And *Matagorda Bay?*" he said.

Chobham stiffened. "She was lost at sea with all hands."

"And all those guns."

"I don't know anything about that!"

"About the guns, or about their loss? Never mind," the stranger said. "Suppose I told you they weren't lost?"

"You astound me! But how would you know that, unless . . ." Chobham's voice trailed off, falling silent.

"Yes?" the stranger prompted. "Unless what?"

The words were pulled from Chobham as if he were reluctant to give them voice.

". . . Unless you have them yourself," he said.

The stranger was silent.

"Do you?" Chobham pressed.

"Don't you know?"

"No."

"I don't think you do, either," the stranger said. "Damn!"

"See here, my man, I can't make heads or tails out of what you're saying."

"Maybe I'd better introduce myself. The name's Slocum."

Arthur Chobham was the investors' man in Aurora. Slocum was supposed to contact him when the *Bay* docked. Of course, things hadn't worked out that way.

Now that he had finally arrived, Slocum went looking for Chobham. First, though, he fixed himself up at Nando's.

Firearms were what Slocum wanted. The shopkeeper's selection was poor. The few firearms he had looked less reliable than knives. The pick of the lot was an old single-barreled shotgun. Nando didn't want to give it up, but Slocum had a bargaining chip. The covetousness with which the servant eyed the obsidian blades proved that they were a valuable commodity. Slocum used that as a lever to pry some concessions out of Nando.

The deal was cut, then the shotgun. The weapon was too unwieldy to go toting around town. Slocum borrowed a hacksaw from Nando. It was rusty and none too sharp. He cut off most of the barrel and stock, reducing it to more manageable dimensions. He must have sweated off half a quart of tequila doing so. Nando sat under the arbor, fanning himself. Slocum filed down the edges of the bore. The weapon was about as long as his forearm.

The trade also included a box of shotgun shells, some clothes, and some small change. Slocum found a shirt and pants close to his size and not too dirty. He put them on. His ragged cut-offs he left on the floor.

"You can burn them," he said.

Nando picked them up, put them aside. "I will sell them."

Slocum also chose a pair of sandals and a broad-brimmed, flat-crowned straw hat. He opened the box of shells and stuffed them in his pockets. He didn't load the sawed-off, not in Nando's presence. That kind of thing makes shopkeepers nervous.

The best dagger he kept for himself. He rolled up his left sleeve, baring his forearm. Using leather thongs, he tied the dagger hilt down to the inside of his arm, covering it with the sleeve. He rigged up a sling for the hand cannon.

At nightfall he took his leave of the shop. He loaded the shotgun. He slung it across his shoulder, hanging muzzle down along his side, hand resting lightly on the chopped stock.

He started toward town. The waterfront had come alive.

Cantinas were bright, smoky, noisy. Sailors and dock hands wandered about in groups, searching for the next drink, the next whore, the next fight. There was no shortage of whores. They thronged the porches and filled the windows of the brothels, calling out to passersby, deriding those who kept going. Lower in the rankings were the legions of street whores, who would do it standing against a wall in an alley for a few centavos. The mix was leavened by the usual assortment of pimps, rogues, and cutthroats.

Slocum kept walking. Soon the noise and lights were behind him. The moon lit the road to town. Breezes blew, bringing the tang of salt sea air.

Ahead, on the left side of the road, stood a darkened shack. Bats flew out from beneath the eaves, flapping into the sky. A knot of figures stood huddled near the corner of the shack.

Slocum kept walking, not slowing his pace. As he neared the house, the figures drifted into the road, blocking the way. Local toughs, four of them. Young, with machetes.

The leader stepped forward, cocky, slapping the flat of the blade in his palm.

Slocum raised the hand cannon, letting them see it as he kept coming.

The leader seemed to shrink into himself. His followers wavered.

Slocum pointed with the shotgun, gesturing for them to be gone. They left at a run, disappearing into the darkness behind the house.

Lights glowed from beyond the next rise: Ciudad Aurora, the seat of local commerce and government.

At its center was the town plaza, a fine, broad square. Grouped around it were old stone buildings with elaborately carved facades. Lights burned in many of the windows. It was easier to do business at night than in the heat of day.

Standing in the shadows, Slocum covered the hand cannon with his shirt. The baggy shirt was worn outside his pants. Loose folds of cloth cloaked the weapon, especially with his arm pressing it to his side. The barrel was cool against his flesh.

The investors had given him two addresses where Chobham might be found: his place of business and his home. His offices were in the Palacio Commercial, where most of the region's important business concerns were headquartered.

The Palacio fronted the square on the north side. Slocum went there, keeping to the sidelines. Chobham didn't advertise himself as a gunrunner; officially, his line was import-export, which was true, as far as it went.

The Palacio was too big, bright, and populated for Slocum to brace Chobham in his office. There were soldiers in the square, too. They idled in an outdoor café, watching the señoritas. A few stood leaning on their rifles, watching the passing parade.

Slocum figured he'd wait until Chobham left the building and pick him up outside. Was he still at work? Slocum parted with most of his few small coins to find the answer. A doorman informed him that Chobham had left for his club some hours ago.

Slocum went to another part of the plaza before asking directions to the Calle de Iguana. The street lay on a rise, midway between the plaza and the church.

Carriages clip-clopped across the square. Slocum would have liked to ride, but he had no money and so must walk. A road rose from the plaza to the church on the hill. Slocum followed it.

Streets branched off on both sides of the road. They were

marked with plaques depicting various objects and animals: a bell, a bird, a flower. The sign identified the street with a picture symbolizing its name.

The Calle de Iguana was on the left. Slocum turned into it. The street was paved with cobblestones; there was money here. It was a short street, with only three houses— big, handsome houses, set well back from the street, each surrounded by extensive grounds and enclosed behind high walls. The front walls began where the curb ended, with no sidewalks. The residents didn't want to encourage outside strollers.

Which house was Chobham's? One house alone had a lightning rod topping its roof, the one at the end of the street. It gleamed in the moonlight, shiny new. Trust a Yankee to do that. Mexican gentry were more conservative, slower to change, unlike their gadget-made neighbors to the north.

The eight-foot wall was topped with spikes and chunks of broken glass mixed in with the cement. It would take more than that to stop Slocum. Like dogs, for instance. Guard dogs would stymie his plan. But there were no dogs. That was a break.

Slocum scaled the wall, dropping into a dark corner of the grounds. There were gardens, winding paths, hedges, flower beds. Figures flitted past lighted windows on the ground floor. Servants, no doubt. Such a house would come complete with its own domestic staff.

No watchmen patrolled the grounds. Slocum went around to the back. The kitchen had its own separate outbuilding, to spare the house the heat of the ovens. Inside, two women did cleaning chores while a man sat and smoked, joking with them. He was the watchman.

Slocum moved on. He came to a terrace. At the other end of it was a row of glass-paned doors. They were all locked. To the left of the terrace, curtains fluttered inside an open window. The room was dark.

Standing on tiptoe, Slocum was just able to reach the windowsill. He pulled himself up and climbed inside. He took pains to avoid bumping anything with the shotgun.

Gauze curtains clung to his face. He brushed them aside, stepping down to the floor. He crouched beside the window, waiting, listening.

It would be too bad if someone was asleep in the room, worse if they were awake.

His eyes were used to the darkness, but there was a limit to what he could see. The room was large, high-ceilinged. Light shone under a door on the opposite wall. There was a smell of leather, wood polish, and paper, lots of paper: books. He was in a study or library of some kind.

Furniture bulked large in the gloom. He padded to the door, taking infinite pains. As a hunter, stealth was second nature to him; he didn't have to think about it.

He stood with his ear to the door. There were random house sounds, the creakings of an old structure settling on its foundations. Occasional distant voices, as of the servants chattering in another wing.

Slocum eased the door open a crack. On the other side was a long hall, lit by wall lamps. The lamps burned low, but they were bright to Slocum, whose eyes were unused to so much light.

The hall was empty. He stuck his head out the door. To the right, the hall stretched into a dark wing. To the left, the hall opened on an airy central space affording a partial view of a winding staircase. Was that the entrance hall opposite the front door?

Light slanted through the open door into the study, falling on a massive wooden desk. Bookcases lined the walls.

There was a standing globe, two armchairs, and a table with straight-backed chairs.

Papers were piled on the desk. Folders, documents, invoices, bills of lading, cargo manifestos. Slocum examined some, holding them up to the light. He was indeed in the home of Arthur Chobham, to whom some of the paperwork was addressed.

More intriguing was the beckoning gleam of highlights in a cut crystal decanter on a sideboard. It was full, too. Slocum lifted the stopper, sniffing the aroma of a truly fine brandy.

He put the brandy and a glass on a little octagonal side table next to an armchair. The armchair had a good line of fire to the door. He poured himself a glassful, closed the door, sat in the chair, and waited.

A cabinet clock ticked off seconds, minutes, hours. Chobham came home around midnight, and came face to face with Slocum.

"But why the elaborate pretense?" Chobham said. "Saying you were from Drago and all that?"

"I had to be sure that you weren't in with the pirates. If you were, you'd have known the true fate of the *Bay* and her cargo," Slocum said.

"A trap, eh? I assume I passed the test."

"You're still alive."

Chobham reached for the brandy. "Do you mind?"

"Help yourself. It's your brandy."

"Ah, yes."

When Chobham set down his empty glass, some color had returned to his face. He leaned forward.

"Do you mean to say that the *Bay*'s been taken by Drago?"

"No," Slocum said.

Chobham sat back. "That's a relief!"

"She's sunk, and her cargo with her."

Chobham took another drink. "The investors won't like this."

"I didn't like it much, myself. Who was supposed to get the guns?"

Chobham fretted. "Well, now, that's a touchy subject. Delicate."

"And I was just starting to like you, too," Slocum said, laying a hand on his gun.

"But I'm sure I can tell you, a confidential agent entrusted by the firm," Chobham said.

It was an old story, old indeed in these waters, where the buccaneer Jean Lafitte had made his last stand after being driven from the Gulf Coast over a half century ago. Old wherever pirates plied their trade. For the truth is that pirates can not long survive on their own, any more than thieves can prosper without buyers of stolen goods.

Such an arrangement had been entered into by the merchants of Aurora. Captain Drago offered rich cargoes at bargain prices. The merchants took them with no questions asked. The shops and market stalls of the port were flush with prize merchandise sold at a fraction of its true worth. The town thrived. Drago took no ships commissioned by the merchants, and all was well.

For a pirate, guns are better than gold. With guns, you can always steal more gold. Drago needed vast quantities of guns, rifles, cannons, powder, and shot. To acquire that kind of hardware, one needs banks, sureties, collateral, letters of credit—all the fussy social mechanisms that a pirate lacks.

Such things were beyond Drago but well within the capacity of the town fathers. Guns for plunder, was Drago's demand: trade prize cargoes for ordnance or feel his wrath.

He could take Auroran ships as easily as any other.

The merchants consented. Still, it was a tricky business. The Mexican government would not look happily on such an exchange. Luckily, there were specialists in such matters, such as the Gulf Coast munitions syndicate represented by the investors Pendleton, Deveraux, and Bliss. They knew how to move armaments without ruffling official feathers.

Chobham was their man in Aurora. He dealt with the merchants. What they did with the guns after they took delivery was none of his business. He didn't ask; they didn't tell. A satisfactory deal. Satisfactory to the investors, too—for a while.

Pirates are true to their nature, which is to raid and plunder. Disturbing rumors began circulating at both ends of the arms pipeline, in Aurora and on the Gulf Coast. Drago was planning to pull a fast one. The investors moved to forestall him.

One of their ploys was to put Slocum aboard the *Bay*. There were other plans, but that was the one that worked.

Chobham didn't see it that way, not yet. He rubbed his face in his hands, blinked bloodshot eyes.

He said, "Now what do we do?"

"Kick their asses," Slocum said.

Not for the first time that night, Chobham stared at him as if he were insane.

"I know where to find the pirates," Slocum said.

13

As a young ensign, Captain Griffith had seen the Battle of Mobile Bay from Admiral Farragut's flagship. Now he commanded the warship U.S.S. *Bellatrix,* standing off Isla Alacran on the Yucatán coast on a gray predawn in late June.

He wore a white cap with a black bill and a navy blue tunic with gold buttons.

Indicating a deck gun, he said, "The honor is yours, Mr. Slocum."

Slocum said, "I believe that honor belongs to Don Felipe."

Griffith nodded. Don Felipe stepped forward. Don Felipe Mendoza, white-haired patriarch, was the father of Pedro Mendoza, who had been lost along with his family on the *Bay.*

The old man was stiff, solemn, dignified. He wore black mourning clothes. He was one of the richest and most respected men in Aurora. Had he traded with the pirates who had slaughtered his son, daughter-in-law, and grandchildren? Slocum didn't want to know.

A retainer stood by in case his strength should fail, but

Don Felipe pulled the firing lanyard by himself.

The cannon thundered.

The shell exploded over the pirate harbor. That was the signal for the bombardment to begin.

The *Bellatrix* fired with all guns blazing.

The investors had friends in the War Department. Naval High Command decided it would be a good idea to have the *Bellatrix* steam down to Yucatán.

Officially, what was now taking place would be described in the captain's log as "target practice on an uninhabited isle."

Officially, the island was uninhabited. It was mapped on the charts but unnamed. Isla Alacran, the local inhabitants called it: Scorpion Island.

Maybe they knew it was a pirate lair but if so, they weren't talking. Slocum was. He described the island and surrounding coastline to the captain and his officers. He was on board for the showdown as was Don Felipe and a group of high Mexican dignitaries, important men in military arms procurement. They wore civilian clothes, though some of them carried themselves in a military manner. They were serious, watchful.

They were getting a first-hand look at some of the finest naval guns made in the United States. Arthur Chobham hovered nearby, order pad in hand. Trust the investors to combine business with revenge!

The cannonade was deafening. Slocum covered his ears with his hands. It didn't help.

He wondered what it sounded like to the pirates.

Drago had been caught napping. He didn't know that Slocum had survived the wreck to testify that the *Bay* had not gone down in a storm, but was, in fact, the victim of mutiny and piracy. He wasn't aware that his secret lair was known or that the *Bellatrix,* on patrol in the Gulf, would steam to his hideout in quick time.

He knew it now.

The black ship rode at anchor in the harbor. The shore was marred by a motley collection of huts and sheds, pirate shantytown. A few gun emplacements dotted the site, but they were unmanned. The pirates were sleeping off last night's drunk. The lookouts, too.

The *Bellatrix* opened up. Her firepower was awesome. Under the barrage, the island shook and smoked like a volcano.

The *Perla Negra* was demasted. Shot after shot tore through her hull. Black sails shrouded the water. The ship lurched under blow after blow. Her magazine blew up, fountaining fire.

That drew cheers on board the *Bellatrix*.

The warship kept firing. The harbor was a mass of smoke and fire. The hulk of the black ship took on water and sank. The stumps of her masts rose above the water.

The barrage stopped.

Slocum couldn't hear a damned thing.

When the smoke cleared, it could be seen that the bombardment had permanently changed the topography of the island's seaward side.

Pulverized remains of pirate town were strewn about the landscape like handfuls of straw and stick matches.

The Mexican dignitaries were impressed, in their solemn, owlish way. They were temporarily deafened, as was Chobham, but that didn't stop him from trying to take orders for the guns.

A landing party was sent ashore to mop up. Slocum was in the first boat, the only civilian in a squad of marines. They had Navy-issue rifles. He had a Winchester and four Colts. Two of the guns were holstered, the others were jammed in his belt.

Scattered sniping erupted from shore. The pirates still had some fight left. More shots crackled, stabbing flames. Bullets whizzed.

The harbor looked like it had been struck by a typhoon. The water was thick with debris. Turbulence rippled from the sunken ship. Thick black smoke rose from burning oil slicks.

Pirate bullets raised waterspouts around the boat. A marine, two thwarts forward of Slocum, was hit in the head.

The boat grounded on shore. The marines jumped out and took cover. Slocum, too. They established a position and returned fire.

The pirates had nothing to lose. If they were taken alive, they had only the gallows to look forward to.

Another boatful of marines landed.

The pirates were trapped rats. The attackers were marines. The leathernecks stormed the beach.

Defense was limited to pockets of resistance. They were contained, isolated, and eliminated in savage face-to-face combat.

Slocum's pistols were devastating in close quarters. Pirates fell under the onslaught.

Amid the chaos there was a familiar sound. He trailed it to its source, where a handful of pirates were making a last stand behind a rocky spur. At their backs was a cliff.

"Idiots," Slocum said.

He got behind a rise where he could fire down at them. He cut loose with his Winchester, shooting into the cleft. The spur covered the pirates in front. He shot at the cliff behind them.

Slugs ricocheted off the wall into the pirates.

One popped up like a startled rabbit. Rector, Drago's top gun. A gun belt was buckled over his priestly garb. A gun was in each hand.

He was hit. That's why he popped up—involuntary reflex action. What a target!

Slocum put one square in Rector's middle. He fell backward, out of sight.

When the shooting stopped, Slocum was the first into the cleft. Bodies sprawled across its sandy floor.

"You cheated the hangman, boys," Slocum said.

One of the dead was Cam Slattery, but Slocum didn't recognize him, not after what the deformed slug of a ricochet had done to his head.

Rector was untouched above the shoulders, his bony skull the color of yellow ivory. His chest was marred by a big red hole. In his hands were two guns. Slocum pried them loose.

They were his guns, the ones he'd left behind in his cabin when he'd gone on deck on the *Bay* for some sea air on the night the pirates came. It seemed ages ago, but it was only a few weeks.

Slocum held the guns, weighing them in his hands, well pleased.

"Knew it was you when I heard you blasting. I know that sound," he said.

He stepped out of the cleft, into the open. The pirates were done. Their ship was sunk, their base destroyed, their forces wiped out. A few had escaped, but not for long.

"That'll teach you not to screw with the man from the sea," Slocum said.

Ahead lay a far more difficult task: squeezing a few dollars more from Pendleton, Deveraux, and Bliss.

Some pirates fled in a handful of skiffs, sailing north. Captain Griffith on the *Bellatrix* lobbed a few shells at them, sinking all but two. Before he could fire another round, a pall of smoke drifted between the warship and the surviving sailboats.

When the smoke cleared, the skiffs were out of range.

"We'll pick them up later," he said.

The northernmost skiff held Captain Drago and a chest of gold. Those who had helped him load and launch the boat died in the shallows with his bullets in their backs.

Far to the rear was a skiff holding Burke Noon, Eel O'Brien, and Mahlon. Their boat had been damaged in the shelling, slowing them down, plus there were three of them.

Drago increased his lead. "He's getting away," O'Brien moaned.

"Shut up and keep baling," Mahlon said.

Noon said nothing. He watched Drago widen the distance between them and steamed. When the skiff finally dwindled into invisibility, he said, "Grrrr."

Drago sailed north, a fair wind at his back. All was not lost. He had a whole skin, a good boat, and gold. Ahead lay Tuluum, Cozumel, and Yalahao. When he reached port, he could disappear into the interior, resurfacing far away, where the name of Drago was unknown.

The devilish warship that had smashed his command was nowhere on the horizon. Neither was the other skiff. The skiff worried him more. His men were in it, and they knew he had gold.

Day became night. The wind fell. Drago drifted. He was tired, hungry, and thirsty. He felt sorry for himself. He lay curled in the bottom of the boat, in a troubled sleep. He awoke in the dead of night, panting, in a cold sweat.

Far out to sea, there were lights. The warship, searching for him? The lights vanished, leaving him wondering if he had dreamed the whole thing.

When the sun came up, there was no sign of the warship or the pursuing skiff.

At midmorning, Drago saw the monster. It lay ahead, athwart his course. It looked like a tortilla, a round, flat disk skimming across the waves—a gray tortilla with a long tail. It was still far away, but closing fast. Drago figured it must be immense, to be visible at such a distance.

The pirate put out to sea to avoid it. It altered its course to intercept him. All the terrors of the deep that he'd sneeringly dismissed now rose up to haunt him—in the flesh. He was in devilfish waters.

Devilfish. The thing was well named. A cunning devil, that moved to block his escape.

Drago changed course again, veering toward shore. Better to run aground than face that thing in open water!

To the west lay an island. He ran for it. Damned if that devilfish wasn't herding him toward it!

Even as he had that thought, the bottom of the boat was ripped out by a coral reef. The sea rushed in. The gold fell overboard.

Water filled the boat to the top of the gunwales, but it didn't sink. It was spiked on the reef. Drago climbed the mast to escape the monster.

The devilfish swam away. Drago was still clinging to his perch when the People of the Sea came to get him.

Hours later, the second skiff came limping onto the scene. A day and night of privation had left its occupants sunk in deep gloom, only lightened by the murderous hatred they now bore toward Drago and each other. Noon would have jettisoned his companions long ago, had he not begun to think of them in terms of steaks and chops. They would have done the same to him, if they could.

That changed when they sighted the wreck.

"Look! Ain't that Drago's boat?" O'Brien said.

"Looks like," Mahlon said.

"Where's Drago?"

"Where's the gold?"

Seabirds circled overhead, screaming. "I can't think in this racket!" O'Brien said.

A swell lifted the boat. Water fizzed, bubbled. The boat was jostled from below.

Mahlon cursed. "We've run aground!"

The boat rose out of the water, supported on the broad back of the devilfish. Its spiked tail struck Mahlon, smashing his skull and spine.

Burke Noon drew his knife and jumped on the monster. He stabbed it deep between the horns, again and again.

The monster spasmed, shedding the boat, which fell on its side, capsizing. O'Brien's scream was silenced when he hit the water.

The creature went berserk. Noon found a handhold in the ancient iron barb stuck in its flesh. His knife ripped and plunged.

The devilfish dove, Noon still clinging to it.

On land, the People of the Sea massed on top of one of the ceremonial mounds. So focused were they on the ritual taking place that they were unaware of the titanic struggle at sea. Even the sentries looked inland to catch some sight of the ceremony.

The tribe was in a sorry state. Many warriors were dead, slain by the Sea Beast. Others nursed broken bones. The old shaman Tata still lived, as did the chief, Yax Balam.

Neither was in any condition to conduct the ceremony. The divine chore was handled by Lady Xoc, who relished her position of power.

Drago was held naked, spread-eagled on the ground. The witch immobilized him by driving stingray spines through his elbows and knees, pinning him.

Then she went to work on him with the knives.

Tata nodded appreciatively. Here was one victim who would not escape the sacrifice!

Drago was a long time dying. The great god Tlaloc would be well pleased. Perhaps he would be merciful and lift his curse.

Red waters churned where the devilfish had gone down. Bobbing among the wreckage of the boat were the bodies of O'Brien and Mahlon. Already the fish had begun to nibble on their eyes.

Burke Noon clung to a spar, alive.

The devilfish was never seen again.

The tide was going out, carrying Noon farther out to sea. He didn't fight it. There was nothing for him on the island. The natives would skin him alive. He'd rather drown.

The spar kept Noon afloat for a day and a night. Blind instinct kept him holding on. Toward the end, he was delirious.

He was rescued by a passing ship. A lookout spotted his head bobbing miles from land, in the empty sea. A boat was lowered to pluck him out of the water.

He came to on deck, lying on his back with a pail of seawater being dumped on his head.

He sat up, spluttering, wiping his face with his hands. Crude laughter brayed around him.

"He rises," somebody said.

He looked around. The crew was a scurvy lot, apes and hyenas in human form. He'd show them who's boss, smash their mocking laughter down their throats, as soon as he got his strength back.

He said, "What ship is this?"

More laughter, mockery.

"What's so damned funny?" Burke Noon said.

A wizened near-dwarf in a filthy apron capered in front of him, filled with sadistic glee.

He cried, " 'Wot ship is this,' 'e says! Wot ship! Hee hee hee!"

"Tell him, Cookie," somebody said.

The Cockney cook leered at Noon.

"Why, you poor fool, you're on the hell-ship *Ghost*, skippered by that bloody devil, Captain Wolf Larsen—the Sea Wolf!"

The crew roared. When the laughter reached its peak, Noon lashed out, kicking out Cookie's feet from underneath him. The Cockney crashed painfully to the deck, crying out.

More laughter, this time at Cookie's expense, with grudging overtones of respect for his tormentor.

Noon climbed to his feet. "Sounds like my kind of ship. I think I'm gonna like this trip!"

A punch in the face sent him flying. Noon was shaken. He'd yet to meet the man who could knock him down with one punch.

He met him now.

Captain Wolf Larsen rubbed his skinned knuckles.

"I'm the one who hands out the beatings on this ship!" he said.

Noon wiped blood from his smashed lips with the back of his hand. "Oh, yeah?"

He popped up, only to be knocked down again. Then Wolf Larsen stomped him flat, beating him within an inch of his life.

The Sea Wolf wasn't even winded.

"Take that bilge rat below," he said. "I'll teach him some manners if it kills him!"

"It might," somebody said.

Ordinarily, Larsen would have flattened the speaker for talking out of turn, but hammering Noon had left him in a good mood.

"Not him. He's tough. He can take it," Larsen said, "and I'm the man who'll dish it out!"

"I think I'm gonna like this trip," he added.

The *Ghost* sailed on.

A special offer for people who enjoy reading the best Westerns published today.

WESTERNS!

NO OBLIGATION

Mail the coupon below

To start your subscription and receive 2 FREE WESTERNS, fill out the coupon below and mail it today. We'll send your first shipment which includes 2 FREE BOOKS as soon as we receive it.